P9-CAS-970

He took her wrist and placed the handcuff around it.

He expected her to put up a fight, but instead, she lay back on the bed. He placed a knee on the bed, leaning over her to fasten the other handcuff to the iron railing of the headboard.

"I'm sorry," he said softly. "I'm only doing this because I can't trust you not to bolt. I meant what I said earlier. It's dangerous out there. You can get seriously hurt on this mountain. I can't allow that to happen."

"No," she whispered. "We can't have you botching an assignment, can we?"

"Stop it, Grace. I know what you're doing, and it won't work."

"Then why are you still here?"

She had a good point. If he had half a brain, he'd move away from her, now, before he remembered the sweetness of her lips, the silkiness of her skin—

Who was he trying to kid? He didn't have to remember, because he'd never forgotten anything about Grace's lovemaking. The way she kissed. The way she touched him. The way she moved against him...

Dear Harlequin Intrigue Reader,

Harlequin Intrigue has such an amazing selection this month, you won't be able to choose—so indulge and buy all four titles!

We're proud to present an exciting new multi-author miniseries, TEXAS CONFIDENTIAL. By day they're cowboys; by night they're specialized government operatives. Men bound by love, loyalty and the law—they've vowed to keep their missions and identities confidential.... Amanda Stevens kicks off the series with *The Bodyguard's Assignment* (#581).

Ruth Glick writing as Rebecca York has added another outstanding 43 LIGHT STREET story to her credits with *Amanda's Child* (#582). When sexy Matt Forester kidnapped Amanda Barnwell from her Wyoming ranch, he swore he was only protecting her. But with her unborn baby's life at stake, could Amanda trust her alluring captor?

We're thrilled to bring you *Safe By His Side* (#583) by brand-new author Debra Webb. This SECRET IDENTITY story is her first ever Intrigue and we're sure you'll love it and her as much as we do. Debra has created The Colby Agency—for the most *private* of investigations—and agent Jack Raine—a man to die for!

In *Undercover Protector* (#584) by Cassie Miles, policewoman Annie Callahan's engagement to Michael Slade wasn't going to lead to the altar. Michael's job was to protect Annie from a deadly stalker. But nothing would protect Michael from heartbreak if he failed....

Next month, join us as TEXAS CONFIDENTIAL continues and a new series, THE SUTTON BABIES by Susan Kearney, begins...and that's just for starters!

Sincerely,

Denise O'Sullivan
Associate Senior Editor
Harlequin Intrigue

THE BODYGUARD'S ASSIGNMENT
AMANDA STEVENS

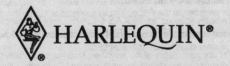

HARLEQUIN®

TORONTO • NEW YORK • LONDON
AMSTERDAM • PARIS • SYDNEY • HAMBURG
STOCKHOLM • ATHENS • TOKYO • MILAN • MADRID
PRAGUE • WARSAW • BUDAPEST • AUCKLAND

Special thanks and acknowledgment are given to
Amanda Stevens for her contribution
to the Texas Confidential miniseries.

ISBN 0-373-22581-4

THE BODYGUARD'S ASSIGNMENT

Visit us at www.eHarlequin.com

Printed in U.S.A.

ABOUT THE AUTHOR

Amanda Stevens has written over twenty novels of romantic suspense. Her books have appeared on several bestseller lists, and she has won Reviewer's Choice and Career Achievement in Romantic/ Mystery awards from *Romantic Times Magazine*. She resides in Cypress, Texas, with her husband, her son and daughter and their two cats.

Books by Amanda Stevens

HARLEQUIN INTRIGUE
373—STRANGER IN PARADISE
388—A BABY'S CRY
397—A MAN OF SECRETS
430—THE SECOND MRS. MALONE
453—THE HERO'S SON*
458—THE BROTHER'S WIFE*
462—THE LONG-LOST HEIR*
489—SOMEBODY'S BABY
511—LOVER, STRANGER
549—THE LITTLEST WITNESS**
553—SECRET ADMIRER**
557—FORBIDDEN LOVER**
581—THE BODYGUARD'S ASSIGNMENT

*The Kingsley Baby
**Gallagher Justice

HARLEQUIN BOOKS
2-in-1 Harlequin 50th Anniversary Collection
HER SECRET PAST

Don't miss any of our special offers. Write to us at the following address for information on our newest releases.

Harlequin Reader Service
U.S.: 3010 Walden Ave., P.O. Box 1325, Buffalo, NY 14269
Canadian: P.O. Box 609, Fort Erie, Ont. L2A 5X3

The Confidential Agent's Pledge

I hereby swear to uphold the law
to the best of my ability; to maintain the
level of integrity of this agency by my
compassion for victims, loyalty to my
brothers and courage under fire.

And above all, to hold all information and
identities in the strictest confidence....

★★★★

CAST OF CHARACTERS

Brady Morgan—An agent for the elite Texas Confidential. His assignment is to protect Grace Drummond at any cost—but can he save her life without compromising his heart?

Grace Drummond—She's running for her life, and the only person who can save her is the man she once betrayed.

Lester Kane—A Dallas drug dealer, he murdered a man in cold blood, and now he will stop at nothing to eliminate the witnesses.

Stephen Rialto—A ruthless businessman pursued by Texas Confidential, he has ties to the Calderone drug cartel.

Helen Parks—Grace's best friend, she warned Grace not to go after a story connecting Lester Kane to Calderone.

Burt Gordon—Grace's boss at the newspaper. Would he sell her out for the sake of a story?

John Kruger—A Department of Public Safety agent who is working closely with Texas Confidential on this case.

Mitchell Forbes—The head of operations of Texas Confidential.

Angeline Drummond—Grace's ailing mother has become an innocent pawn in a very dangerous game.

Prologue

"I can't believe you're going through with this. Do you know what those people will do if they catch you? They're killers, Grace. Vicious, cold-blooded murderers."

Her friend's warning echoed inside Grace Drummond's head as she tried to settle into a more comfortable position behind the giant pallets of carpet rolls. The fibers made her want to sneeze, and even though she was alone in the warehouse, she pinched her nose painfully until the urge passed.

She pressed the button on her watch to light the dial and noted the time. One forty-three. According to her contact inside Lester Kane's operation, the meeting between Kane and a representative from Rialto Industries was set for 2:00 a.m., a time when most people would be home sleeping. Grace had seventeen minutes, less than half an hour, to hightail it out of there, but she knew she wasn't going to run. As a reporter for the *Dallas Examiner*, she'd been in hairy situations before. This one was no different from a dozen others.

Right.

"Don't you remember what happened to those DEA agents who came up against the Calderone drug cartel down in Mexico? They cut out their eyes and gave them to the local witch doctor. I shudder to think what they did with the rest of them."

Grace didn't need Helen Parks's graphic reminder to know she was walking a fine line between bravery and stupidity. If she got the story, she'd be able to prove Lester Kane's connection to Rialto Industries, a Houston-based oil company with secret ties to the Calderone drug cartel in Mexico. Calderone's entire Gulf Coast operation could be jeopardized because once Grace got the goods on Kane, he'd cooperate with the authorities to save his own sleazy hide—if the police could keep him alive long enough.

Of course, if she didn't get the story—if she was caught—Grace figured it wasn't much worse being dead and stupid than being just plain dead. At least she would have tried to make things right.

But no matter how much she might wish to, Grace knew she couldn't go back and erase the mistakes she'd made five years ago. Because of her, Lester Kane had eluded a sting operation the Narcotics Division of the Dallas Police Department had been working on for months. And because of that, a cop named Brady Morgan had walked out of her life forever.

Tonight, she finally had a chance to make amends

for what she'd done, but she doubted it would matter to Brady. He'd told her back then he never wanted to see her again, and he'd kept his word. In the years since he'd left town, Grace had not heard one word from him.

Glancing around, she assured herself once more that she was well-hidden. The warehouse, one of several owned by Kane, was stacked with rolls of carpeting piled more than fifteen feet high. A row of dirty windows beneath the ceiling allowed in a pale dripping of moonlight, just enough so that once Grace had become accustomed to the gloom, she could make out shapes and silhouettes but little else.

Her contact had left a side door unlocked near the back of the warehouse, and Grace had used her flashlight only long enough to plant a remote microphone and then find a hiding place. There was nothing more she could do now but relax and wait, two things she wasn't terribly good at.

The minutes crept by. Grace glanced at her watch again. Nearly two. Any moment now…

As if on cue, the overhead door rumbled open, startling her so violently she almost dropped her tape recorder.

Quickly she checked to make sure the switch was on, then settled back, willing the beat of her heart to slow. Her contact inside Kane's operation was a man named Alec Priestley, who not only worked for Kane, but had been his childhood buddy. They'd grown up together in Grapevine, a small community north of Dallas. Kane had been the best man at

Priestley's wedding. Grace had no reason to trust Priestley except for what her own instincts told her about him. He wanted out. She'd seen the desperation in his eyes, could almost smell his fear when he'd approached her with his proposition. Either he was telling her the truth, or he was a very good actor. In a few short minutes, she would know which.

A black Mercedes sedan swept silently into the warehouse. Instinctively Grace shielded her eyes from the glare of the headlights as she scrunched lower into her hiding place. A second car followed immediately, this one a silver Jaguar coupe that Grace knew belonged to Kane.

As soon as the overhead door closed, the lights on the Mercedes were turned off and three men in dark suits got out. Kane and Priestley climbed out of the Jag and approached the other three warily. They all met in the amber glow of the Jaguar's parking lights—the only illumination in the warehouse.

Grace shifted her weight until she could see through a narrow opening between the carpet rolls. She recognized Kane and Priestley, but the other three were unfamiliar to her. She thought one of them might be Stephen Rialto, but he kept his face turned away from her. She had to imagine the cruel set of his mouth, the coldness in his eyes. From everything she'd learned about Rialto, she suspected he would slit her throat—or order it done—without batting an eye if he found her there.

He was flanked on either side by the other two

men who had gotten out of the Mercedes. Grace couldn't see their features clearly, either, but she had the impression of dark eyes and swarthy complexions. Bodyguards, she decided. Trained thugs whose orders were to shoot first and ask questions later.

Her gaze shifted to Priestley. He stood at the periphery of the group, white-faced and jittery as he glanced around the warehouse.

Come on, Grace urged. *Stay cool. Don't give us away.*

She prayed the others would be so busy forging their unholy alliance they wouldn't notice his nervousness. But neither Lester Kane nor Stephen Rialto had gotten as far as he had by being careless. Grace couldn't hear much of what was being said, but she could tell they were all tense.

Kane was talking in low, persuasive tones, and Grace strained to hear him. The other man's voice rose as he responded tersely, "Then prove your loyalty, Kane. We have to know we can trust you."

"If that's what it takes, then so be it," Kane said.

From her vantage, Grace saw what none of the others could see. Unobtrusively, Kane reached around and drew a gun from the waistband of his trousers. Grace had only a split second to wonder why Rialto's men didn't react before Kane swung his arm toward Priestley. He fired the silenced weapon twice. A soft *spit, spit,* and Alec Priestley, husband, businessman, father of two, crashed back into a wooden pallet, his face and chest a crimson explosion.

Grace clapped a hand over her mouth to keep from gasping in shock. She watched in horror as the other men began to swing back to their cars. "Torch the place!" someone ordered.

One of the bodyguards grabbed a gas can from the trunk of the Mercedes and began dousing the carpet rolls while Kane reversed the Jag from the warehouse. The other two men climbed into the Mercedes and followed. The first bodyguard finished his job, then tossed the empty gas can aside. Running to the open doorway, he stood gazing around for a moment before flicking a lit match toward a trail of fuel on the floor. Then he disappeared through the opening, and the door immediately closed.

As the ribbon of fire raced toward the drenched carpet rolls, Grace grabbed her recorder and scrambled through the narrow channel between the pallets. The natural carpet fibers would burn quickly, but the synthetic rolls were potentially even more dangerous. The nylon would melt and smolder, causing black smoke to build inside the warehouse. The acrid smell already burned her eyes and throat.

The side door was somewhere just ahead of her. *Don't panic,* she told herself. She had plenty of time to get out. Just a few more yards…a few more feet… a few more inches…

Her hand closed around the metal knob and she pulled. When the door wouldn't budge, she gave it a fierce yank, and then another and another, each more desperate than the last until she realized the exit had been padlocked from the outside. Other than the overhead door through which the cars had driven, there was no other way out of the warehouse.

Grace whirled to retrace her steps, but the flames had spread quickly. The entire warehouse was ablaze, the smoke nearly opaque. In another few moments, she would be overcome.

A few yards in front of her, the smoke curled upward, fanned by a breeze. Grace's gaze followed the writhing trail, and she realized that a pane in one of the windows was missing. The night air was drawing the thick haze like a flue. It was also showing her what might be another way out.

But the windows were a good twenty feet from the ground. Grace wasn't at all certain she could reach them. Knowing it was her only hope, she began to climb the wooden pallets, her lungs searing in agony. She wouldn't let herself look down, or think about the flames that were licking toward her, the rolls of carpeting that were melting beneath her feet.

She wouldn't contemplate the reality that if she died in this warehouse, she would never be able to redeem herself in Brady Morgan's eyes....

Chapter One

The landscape was as vast as it was empty, a waste-
land of rugged plains made even more bleak by the
dead of winter. In the distance, mist settled over
the craggy peaks of the Davis Mountains, softening
the jagged edges until gray rock melded almost
seamlessly with slate sky.

Brady Morgan huddled in his sheepskin coat as
he watched a hawk circle overhead. He'd been living and working on the Smoking Barrel Ranch for
almost five years now, but he still hadn't gotten used
to the loneliness of the place.

West Texas was a world unto itself, and he
guessed he was still a city boy at heart. He'd grown
up in a rough area of Dallas, had been a street cop
for several years before joining the Narcotics Division. During those years, he'd seen the worst human
nature had to offer, and sometimes the best, but
nothing he'd experienced as a cop had ever made
him as aware of his own mortality, of his insignifi-

cance in the whole scheme of things, as the boundless isolation of the ranch.

He'd been riding fence all morning, and in spite of the thick cowhide gloves he wore, his hands were numb from the cold. The white ranch house was hardly more than a speck on the endless horizon, but Brady could imagine the curl of smoke from the chimneys, the rich aroma of Rosa's strong coffee permeating the warm kitchen. He gave Rowan a nudge, urging the red chestnut homeward across the rocky turf.

They'd stayed out too long. Rowan's breath rolled from his nostrils like steam hissing from a locomotive, and the dull ache in Brady's knee had turned into searing pain. But he wouldn't give in to that pain. He'd had enough drugs and doctors to last him a lifetime, and besides, none of them could fix what really ate at him anyway. A shot-up knee would heal in time, but a young woman he'd sworn to protect couldn't be brought back to life.

Idly, he watched a tumbleweed roll across the frozen tundra in front of him, but in his mind's eye he pictured a cloud of dark hair and soft, soulful eyes. Rachel had been a good person, but she'd gotten herself mixed up in a bad business. A nasty business. When she'd wanted out, her ex-lover, a Houston drug lord named Stephen Rialto, hadn't thought twice about sending his goons to storm the safe house where Brady had taken her until she could testify. Brady's leg had been shot to hell in the raid, but Rachel had been killed. She'd died in his arms.

The burning throb in his leg was a grim reminder of how powerful and dangerous Stephen Rialto had become. Obviously he had a mole somewhere—in the FBI, the Department of Public Safety, maybe even in the Texas Confidential. But Brady didn't think the latter was too likely. The Confidential was a tight-knit organization. He knew all the agents personally. In some ways, they'd become his family. He couldn't—wouldn't—believe that one of them had betrayed him. But then, betrayal could come where and when you least expected it. He'd learned that lesson a long time ago.

As he drew near the sprawling, two-story ranch house, he saw the front door open, and a figure stepped out onto the wide front porch. She waited until Brady had dismounted and tied Rowan to the cedar rail outside the bunkhouse before running lightly down the porch steps.

Protected from the cold by a dark blue parka, Penny Archer strode toward him with purpose, the flat soles of her boots thudding on the hard ground. The hood of her coat hid her expression, but something about the way she hurried toward him struck Brady as ominous. It was as if she'd been waiting for him, watching for him from one of the front windows of the ranch house.

As she approached, Rowan began to prance and snort, bucking at the reins wrapped around the cedar rail.

Penny said irritably, "Why do you keep that damn horse? He's dangerous."

"He's a pussycat around anyone but you," Brady teased, his breath frosting on the cold air. "You bring out the beast in him."

Penny gave him a dour look behind her wire-rimmed glasses. "God knows I should be used to working with animals."

Brady grinned. Penny's disdain for the agents—all male—with whom she worked was legendary. She didn't take much guff from any of them, except maybe for Rafe Alvarez. She tried to pretend his good-natured ribbing didn't get to her, but Brady had seen the way she looked at the agent when she thought no one was watching. He wondered if Rafe had any idea Penny was in love with him. He wondered if Penny even knew.

"Mitchell wants to see you ASAP," she told him.

"What's up?"

She shrugged. "How should I know? He never tells me anything. I'm just the gofer around here."

Yeah, right. Penny was more than that and she knew it. As Mitchell Forbes's assistant, she kept the ranch and the Texas Confidential running as smoothly as a well-tuned engine. She knew everything there was to know about each case they took on, and her air of innocence this morning didn't wash. A bad sign that she was keeping something from him, Brady thought.

"I'll be in as soon as I see to Rowan," he told her.

She shrugged again. "Okay, fine. Suit yourself.

Mitchell said for you to come *immediately*, but it's your hide, not mine. I'm just the messenger.''

Brady's foreboding deepened as he led the horse toward the barn. Mitchell Forbes wasn't one for idle conversation. If he wanted to see Brady this urgently, it was because he had an assignment for him. And Brady wasn't ready for that.

After Rachel, he wasn't sure he ever would be.

BY THE TIME Brady got to the ranch house, the rest of the agents had already assembled in the war room—that section of the special-built basement which had become Command Central for the organization. The Confidential was not a secret group per se, but as a specialized division of the Department of Public Safety, they worked cases that were highly sensitive. Discretion was vital, literally a matter of life and death, and the possibility of a mole, someone who had tipped off Rialto to Rachel's whereabouts—who might also be responsible for the recent disappearance of one of their agents—had them all concerned.

"Señor Brady!" Rosa, the Smoking Barrel's housekeeper, bustled into the library as Brady summoned the elevator.

For security purposes, the elevator was hidden behind a bookshelf that slid away with the push of a button, then rolled back into place once the elevator was activated from inside the car. The high-tech and secretive nature of the organization always made Brady feel a little ridiculous, a little too 007-ish. He was basically just a cop, although the undercover work wasn't that different from the assignments he'd had as a narc. But that was a long time ago. A part of his life he didn't much like to think about.

Gratefully, he accepted the steaming mug of coffee the housekeeper handed him. "You read my mind, Rosa."

She beamed. "You've been out in the cold all morning. You need some of Rosa's good coffee to warm you up. I make it just the way you like. Black and strong enough to grow hair."

"I think you mean strong enough to put hair on my chest," he said dryly.

She muttered something in Spanish Brady couldn't quite catch. He sampled the bitter, chicory brew which no one else at the Smoking Barrel could abide. Wusses, he thought scornfully. Wranglers and secret agents aside, a man wasn't a man until he could drink a cup of coffee strong enough to…grow its own hair.

Rosa planted a hand on one generous hip as she waited for his response.

"*Perfecto*. Rosa, I do believe I'd ask you to marry me if I didn't think you were sweet on ole Slim."

At the mention of the grizzled ranch hand, Rosa let out a string of rapid-fire Spanish which Brady suspected might have not only grown hair but curled it as well, had he been able to keep up. A few English words were intermixed, something about an old flirt or an old fart, or a combination of the two.

Sipping his coffee, Brady rode the elevator down

to the basement. He was greeted warmly by the other agents, and in spite of his trepidation at this impromptu meeting, he couldn't help responding to the camaraderie. He hadn't been a part of a family since he was a kid, but in the nearly five years he'd been with the Confidential, he'd become closer to the other agents than he had with anyone since his mother died.

And Mitchell Forbes, the white-haired ex-Texas Ranger who had been in the Hanoi Hilton with Brady's father, had become, if not a surrogate parent, at least a man Brady looked up to and admired. Mitchell had recruited Brady at a time when his confidence was badly shaken—a time not unlike now.

He took a seat at the conference table next to Jake Cantrell, a former FBI agent. "What's going on?"

Jake shrugged. "Beats me, but it must be something big. Mitchell looks worried."

Brady had to agree. Normally, Mitchell Forbes was a man to be reckoned with on the range or in the war room, but today his face was drawn with tension. As he sat at the head of the conference table, gazing at the assembled agents, his thumb worked back and forth on an ornate silver lighter, a sure sign of his anxiety.

A man Brady didn't recognize was seated to Mitchell's right. He studied an open folder on the table in front of him, and unlike the others, he hadn't glanced up when Brady entered the basement.

Rafe Alvarez, ever irreverent no matter what the situation, said into the waiting silence, "Hey, Mitchell, what happened? Maddie stand you up last night?''

Maddie Wells, a widow who owned the neighboring spread, was something of a sore subject with Mitchell, and when Cody Gannon gave a hoot of laughter at Rafe's impertinence, Mitchell pinned him with an icy glare. Cody's smile faded, and for a long moment, the two of them remained locked in a silent battle of wills until finally the younger man glanced away.

Brady didn't understand why Mitchell always picked on Cody. He was the youngest Confidential, and basically a good kid, even if he was a little on the wild side. But, hell, they'd all been young once. And if local talk was to be believed, Mitchell Forbes had sown his share of wild oats.

There'd been a few times when Brady had been tempted to point out that fact to Mitchell, to ask him to lighten up on the kid, but it wasn't any of his business. And Cody was just muleheaded enough to take offense at the interference. Whatever burr the two of them had under their saddles, Brady figured they'd have to work it out for themselves. Besides, he had his own problems to deal with.

Mitchell flicked open the lighter and touched the flame to the clipped end of his cigar. The puffs of smoke drifting through the room signaled the meeting had come to order. Everyone grew deadly serious, the absence of their colleague, who had vanished a month ago while investigating the Calderone drug cartel, uppermost on their minds these days.

"There's still been no word of Daniel," Mitchell said gravely, referring to the missing agent. "But we may finally have a break in the case."

Beside him, Brady sensed Jake's sudden tension. Jake had a long history with both Rialto and Calderone. They'd taken something from him that he could never get back, and Brady alone knew that this case wasn't just personal for Jake. It was a vendetta.

Jake leaned forward in his chair, his gaze riveted on Mitchell. "What kind of break?"

Mitchell nodded to the man seated next to him. "This is John Kruger. He's assigned to the HIDTA office in Houston, but he's also worked closely with the drug squads in El Paso." The High Intensity Drug Trafficking Area, or HIDTA, was a task force set up by the Narcotics Service of the Department of Public Safety. The agents who worked in this area were highly trained in undercover, surveillance, and interception. Brady glanced at Kruger with new respect.

"John will be our point man at the DPS," Mitchell continued. "I'll let him fill you in on the details."

For the first time, Kruger looked up from the folder he'd been studying, his gaze cool and assessing as he glanced around the table. He was about Brady's age—thirty-five—with brown hair and blue eyes so light, they almost appeared transparent. The illusion was a little disconcerting, and as his gaze met Brady's for an instant, Brady experienced a twinge of unease.

"I'll get right to the point, gentlemen." Kruger closed the folder and stood. "We think we've found a way to get to Stephen Rialto through a Dallas drug dealer named Lester Kane."

This time, it was Brady who tensed. Lester Kane was *his* old nemesis, a devious bastard who had eluded the Dallas P.D.—and Brady—for too many years. "What's Kane got to do with Rialto?" he asked sharply.

He could feel Mitchell's steely gaze on him. Besides Jake, Mitchell was the only other person in the room who knew the whole story behind Brady's sudden departure from the Dallas police force.

"We believe Kane has forged an alliance with Rialto," Kruger explained. "In recent months, southeastern Texas has become the hottest transit zone for illegal drugs in this country. The Calderone cartel has become second only to the Juarez cartel in terms of volume. We estimate that each cartel ships upward of two hundred million dollars worth of drugs across the border a week. As a distributor for Calderone, Rialto's business has literally exploded, and he's looking to branch out, which is where Kane comes in. He wants the Dallas and Fort Worth area, and with Rialto's help, he's already muscled out most of his competition.

"We believe Rialto and Kane are positioning themselves to take over Calderone's entire southwestern operation. The DPS and the DEA have monitored a flurry of recent meetings in both Dallas and Houston between the two organizations. One of those meetings took place the night before last in a warehouse owned by Kane. The place was torched afterward, and a body was found in the rubble. The victim has been identified as Alec Priestley, an associate of Kane's. He was shot twice at close range before the fire was set. There was a witness.''

A witness.

Brady had a sinking feeling in the pit of his stomach. He had a score to settle with both Lester Kane and Stephen Rialto, but he didn't like the sound of this. Witness protection, the kind neither the U.S. Marshals Service nor the DPS was willing to provide, was Brady's specialty. Or had been, until Rachel.

"Kane and Priestley go back a long way," Kruger continued. "They both started dealing in college, and afterward, Kane expanded the operation. Priestley went on to law school, but a few years later, he rejoined Kane in the business. Priestley was always the nervous type, but he went along with whatever Kane wanted so long as they kept the operation low-profile. It was a way to rake in a lot of extra cash, selling mainly to friends and clients, people he could trust.

"Then Kane became involved with Rialto and the Calderone drug Mafia, and the business, which had been a sideline for Priestley up until then, got serious. Priestley got scared. He wanted out. He started feeding information to a local reporter about Kane's connection to Rialto and Calderone, and he arranged for her to be in the warehouse the night he was killed. Not only did she witness Priestley's murder, but she got everything on tape, including the voice of a man we think is Stephen Rialto.'' Kruger paused dramatically, his gaze slipping from one agent's face to the next. "Kane is the way we get to Rialto.''

"So where do we come in?'' Rafe asked.

"Dallas P.D. has requested through the DPS that your organization handle the protection.'' Kruger's gaze stopped on Brady. "We have to assume the witness is refusing to cooperate. She made contact with the police early yesterday morning, but since then, she's gone underground. No one has seen or heard from her in over twenty-four hours, but one thing's certain. If we don't find her before Kane does, she's a dead woman. The Dallas P.D. are moving to arrest Kane, but without her statement or that tape, they'll never make the charges stick.''

"Are you sure she's still alive?'' Jake asked.

"By all indications, she's extremely resourceful. We have every reason to believe she's alive and well, at least for the time being. But she can't hide forever. Not with Calderone and Rialto backing Kane.''

Brady hadn't said a word for several minutes, but the bad feeling he'd experienced earlier had grown into a full-blown premonition. He knew what was coming.

"Who is this reporter?'' he asked quietly.

"She works for a small paper called the *Examiner*. Her name is Grace Drummond."

Even after all these years, the mere mention of her name was like the twisting of a knife blade in Brady's gut.

"Her disappearance could have more to do with her desire to get a hot story than anything else," he suggested, not bothering to disguise the bitterness he still felt toward Grace Drummond.

"We've considered that, of course," Kruger agreed. "But as I said, she did initially make contact with the police. When they arrived at her apartment, the place had been ransacked. We figure she panicked. She realized the tape is her only insurance policy against Kane. Once she gives it up, there's nothing stopping him from killing her. Your job is to find her before Kane does and...convince her to accept your protection until she can testify against him."

There was no mistaking his emphasis on the word "convince." The subtle implication was to use whatever means necessary to bring her in. That, at least, had possibilities, Brady thought perversely.

"I'll do it," Jake volunteered.

But Mitchell shook his head. "We need Brady on this one. The doctors have given him the okay to return to active duty, and he's the protection expert. Besides, DPS thinks she's still in the Dallas area, right?" When Kruger nodded, Mitchell said, "Brady, you know that city better than any of us. If anyone can find her, you can. Penny's already made all the arrangements.'' He stubbed out his cigar, signaling the conclusion of the meeting. The other agents rose to leave. Until further notice, they'd all resume their duties on the ranch.

Kruger remained for a moment, speaking in low tones to Mitchell. They appeared to be arguing, and then Kruger grabbed up his folder, stuffed it into his briefcase, and with one final glance at Brady, stalked from the room.

For a moment, Brady said nothing, then he got up and walked to the end of the conference table, planting his hands flat on the surface as he leaned toward Mitchell.

''What were you and Kruger arguing about?''

Mitchell shrugged. ''That's nothing for you to worry about. I don't always see eye-to-eye with Austin,'' he said. ''You know that.''

''Kruger doesn't want me for this job, does he?''

Mitchell glanced up at him. ''It doesn't matter what Kruger wants. I'm in charge of the Confidential.''

''Have you ever considered that he may have a point?''

''Meaning?''

Brady straightened, taking pressure off his knee. ''Have you forgotten what happened to the last woman you sent me out to protect?''

Mitchell's gaze narrowed on him. ''I haven't forgotten, but maybe it's time you did.''

''A woman died last year because of me,'' Brady said grimly. ''I'm not likely to forget it.''

"That's a load of crap and you know it." Mitchell took out another cigar, but he didn't light up. He pointed the end at Brady. "You put your life on the line to protect your witness. You almost died. No one could have done more."

"Are you sure about that? How do you know Rachel Hayes isn't dead because of something I did or didn't do?"

"You think I haven't been where you are?" Mitchell demanded. "I've been there plenty of times. I know what you're going through, but it comes with the territory. You were a cop for a lot of years, Brady. You know as well as I do that bad things happen and good people die. We're not God. We can't save them all. But we do what we can."

He paused, wrapping his hands around the silver head of his cane. He pushed himself up until he stood eye level with Brady. "There's a woman out there somewhere, running for her life. She's the one who needs you now. She's the one you should be thinking about. If you don't do what you can to save her, then it's going to be Grace Drummond's death on your conscience. No matter what she did to you in the past, I don't think you want that."

He was right about that. Brady didn't want anything bad to happen to Grace, he just never wanted to see her again.

But Mitchell was right about something else, too. Rachel's death would haunt Brady for the rest of his life, but Grace's death...

Grace's death on his conscience might very well destroy him.

Chapter Two

Through her dark glasses, Grace anxiously scoured the pedestrian traffic on Market Street. A cold front had moved in earlier, and she sat shivering in the lightweight denim jacket she'd hastily purchased yesterday, after she'd decided to go underground. Actually, it hadn't been a decision so much as a necessity. She had to lay low if she wanted to stay alive. If she wanted to keep her mother alive.

At the thought of Angeline, bitter tears stung Grace's eyes, but she blinked them away. She couldn't break down now. She had to stay focused, in control. She had to have a plan.

If only there was someone she could call, someone she could turn to. Someone she could trust. But there wasn't. After everything that had happened since two o'clock yesterday morning, when she'd narrowly escaped that burning warehouse, Grace knew she could rely on no one but herself. No one could save her mother but her.

She suppressed another shiver as she tried to fight

back her mounting despair. It was too cold to be seated outside, but she hadn't wanted to be trapped inside the café. Out here, even with the coming darkness, she could at least watch the street.

Picking up her cup of coffee, she cradled the warmth in her hands as she scanned her surroundings. A horse-drawn carriage ambled down the street, stirring bittersweet memories of the last time she and her mother had taken a carriage ride together. Angeline had been in the early stages of Alzheimer's then, with only the occasional memory lapse to remind them that one day soon, there would be no such outings.

Grace's mother had always loved coming to Dallas's West End, perusing the shops and dining in the converted warehouses. As Grace sat watching the street she and her mother had strolled together so many times in the past, a sense of desperation stole over her. *Where are you?* she cried silently. *What have they done to you?*

Yesterday morning, just hours after Grace had fled the warehouse, she'd gone home from a meeting with Burt Gordon, her boss at the *Examiner,* to find that her apartment had been sacked. As she'd stood gazing at the wreckage of her personal belongings, her cellular phone had rung. When Grace answered, a male voice on the other end said, "Grace Drummond?"

Something about the way he spoke her name made her blood go cold. "Yes?"

"You have something I want."

"Who is this?"

"You know who I am."

"Kane?" His name was barely a whisper on her lips.

He gave a low laugh. "I understand you've gotten pretty chummy with one of my colleagues. Unfortunately, Alec met his untimely demise earlier this morning, but then, you already know that, don't you?"

Grace's heart thundered in her ears. How had Kane known about her association with Priestley? Had Priestley talked? Had he sold her out before he died?

She swallowed, trying to calm her racing pulse. "What do you want?"

"Don't play dumb. You know what I want." Kane paused. "Tell me something, Grace. How long has it been since you talked to your mother?"

The connection had been severed with a soft click, leaving Grace clinging to the telephone with a horrible dread. She'd immediately dialed the number of the nursing home where her mother lived, only to have the director tell her that Angeline had been transported by ambulance a short while ago to another facility as per Grace's written request.

Grace had given no such instructions, and when she'd called the new facility, they'd never heard of her or her mother. By that time, Grace was in her car, racing toward the nursing home. When her cell phone rang again, she lifted it to her ear without saying a word, knowing instinctively who was on the other end.

"Now I have something you want."

Grace's stomach rolled sickeningly. "Don't hurt her. I swear to God, if you hurt her in any way—"

"Cut the dramatics," Kane said cruelly. "We both know you aren't in any position to make threats. From here on out, I call the shots."

When Grace didn't respond, he laughed. "You're in over your head, little girl. I've got people in places you can't begin to imagine. You talk to a friend, I'll know it. You talk to the cops again—I'll know that to. You understand?"

Grace understood. Only too well. Her hand shook as she gripped the phone. In the last five years, she'd done a lot of research on the drug trade. Drug lords spent millions of dollars a year to keep cops on their side. Obviously, Kane was no exception.

"You want to keep your mother alive, you keep your mouth shut." His voice lowered dangerously. "If I so much as smell a cop nosing around that nursing home, or anywhere else, she's a dead woman."

Grace squeezed her eyes closed in fear. "Tell me what to do." But even in her state of terror, she knew she was dealing with a man she couldn't trust. A cold-blooded murderer. It would take equal cunning to get her mother out of this alive.

"You keep that phone close by, you hear? I'll be in touch. We'll set up a drop. Your mother for that tape."

"When—"

The phone had gone dead in Grace's ear, and she hadn't heard from Kane since. It had been over twenty-four hours.

She knew what he was doing. He was making her sweat. Wearing her down. Making her so desperate to save her mother that she would get careless.

Her fingers trembled around the now lukewarm cup of coffee as she contemplated her dilemma. Her frail, beautiful mother was being held hostage for the tape that could put Kane away forever, and possibly incriminate Stephen Rialto. That tape—and Grace's silence—was the only thing that could save Angeline's life.

But Grace knew once Kane had what he wanted, he would come after them. He wouldn't take a chance on her silence, and she had to be ready. Once the exchange was made, she and Angeline would have to disappear forever.

Her heart quickened as she spotted a familiar figure crossing the street toward her. Even in the deepening twilight, she could see Helen Parks's agitation in the way she walked, in the nervous way she glanced over her shoulder from time to time. She was warmly dressed in a long wool coat and leather gloves, and a metal briefcase swung at her side.

Helen paused on the sidewalk in front of the café, her gaze meeting Grace's for an instant before she disappeared inside, only to emerge moments later on the patio. She sat down at the table with Grace and placed the briefcase on the floor between them.

One leather-clad hand reached for Grace's on the table. Her dark eyes searched Grace's face. "God, are you all right? I've been worried out of my mind ever since Burt told me what happened."

"Burt?" Absently, Grace pulled her hand away, entangling her fingers together in her lap. "What did he say?"

"He's worried about you, too. He said you called him night before last and had him meet you at the office. He said you were scared to death and that you were going to the police with a tape you'd made." Helen glanced around the almost deserted patio. "Grace, what's going on? What have you gotten yourself into? It has something to do with the Calderone drug cartel, doesn't it?"

"In a roundabout way," Grace admitted. She scanned the patio, too. "You remember the night I staked out the warehouse? They murdered a man, Helen. My contact. Alec Priestley. I saw it. I got the whole thing on tape. They set the warehouse on fire, and I barely made it out. I didn't know what to do at first, so I called Burt and asked him to meet me at the office. We talked about the situation for a long time. He wanted me to turn over the tape to him for safekeeping, but I'd already stashed it. And by that time, I knew I had to go to the police. I mean...I'd witnessed a murder. What else could I do?"

Helen's gaze looked stricken. "I told you not to go there that night, remember? I warned you what kind of people they were."

"I know. And believe me, I wish I'd listened to you," Grace said grimly.

"What happened with Burt?"

"He stormed out of the office when I refused to turn over the tape. I used his phone to call the police. I talked to a detective, told him I'd witnessed a murder. I could finger Lester Kane and possibly Stephen Rialto, and I had the whole thing on tape. I asked him to meet me at my apartment later that morning so that I could throw some things together. I knew I'd be taken into protective custody, and I had to take care of some business first. Besides, I had no reason to believe I was in any danger. I mean no one even knew about me, right? Or the tape? At least, that's what I thought. But when I got home a few hours later, my apartment had been tossed. Someone was already looking for that tape, Helen. Kane already knew about me."

Helen's dark eyes widened in fear. "But how did he find out so quickly? You didn't tell anyone except Burt and the police—" She stopped short. Her gloved hand went to her mouth. "You're not saying you think Burt—"

"I don't know. But Kane found out about me somehow."

"Maybe he already knew. Let's think about this for a minute." Helen stared at the street pensively as she tucked her short, dark hair behind her ears. "Your contact—this Alec Priestley—he could have gotten cold feet and told Kane himself. At any rate,

Kane must have suspected him. Why else would he have killed him?''

Grace shrugged helplessly. "I've been over and over this in my head, Helen. Priestley left a door in the warehouse unlocked for me that night so that I could get in and hide, but after the fire started, I couldn't get out. Someone had padlocked the door from the outside, which means someone already knew I was in there. I was supposed to die in that fire.'' She paused when Helen gasped. Grace leaned toward her slightly, lowering her voice even more. "Burt knew I was going to the warehouse that night. He also knew Priestley was my contact.''

Helen looked a little dazed. "I just don't buy it. I refuse to believe Burt would sell you out like that. Not even for a story. He wouldn't be in cahoots with a drug dealer. No way.''

"I don't want to believe it, either, but who else could have known?''

"Well,'' Helen said slowly. "There was me.''

Grace met her gaze in shock. "*You?* You wouldn't—''

"No,'' Helen cut in. "I wouldn't betray you. Of course not. But I'm just saying other people knew besides Burt. He can be ruthless when he's after a story, but he's not a criminal. I think deep down you know that.''

Grace didn't know what to think. It wasn't like Burt Gordon hadn't betrayed her before. It wasn't like he was above doing something underhanded.

"What about the police?'' Helen asked. "You

said you called and told them everything. A cop on the take isn't unheard of.''

''I know that.'' Kane had hinted as much when he'd called her. *''I've got people in places you can't begin to imagine.''*

Grace shuddered, glancing around the darkened streets.

''The cops have been all over your office,'' Helen said. ''Going through your files, reading your phone messages. I wouldn't be surprised if they've put out an APB on you.''

Grace wouldn't be surprised, either. She was their key witness, after all. ''Did they take anything from my files?''

''I don't know. But a detective came by my office asking questions.''

''What kind of questions?''

Helen shrugged. ''The usual stuff—if I'd heard from you. Where I thought you might be.''

''What did you tell him?'' Grace asked anxiously.

''The truth. I *hadn't* heard from you then, and I didn't know where to find you.'' She leaned across the table toward Grace. ''What are you going to do?''

''I'm not sure,'' Grace admitted. ''Lay low for a few days until I can figure things out.'' She hadn't told anyone, even Helen, about her mother's kidnapping. The last thing she needed was a horde of cops descending on the nursing home, alerting Kane that she'd talked. *''You talk to a friend, I'll know it. You talk to the cops again…I'll know that, too.''*

Helen nudged the briefcase toward her. "I got the money you asked for. As much as I could on such short notice."

"I don't know how I can ever thank you," Grace told her. "I'll pay you back as soon as I can."

Helen's brown eyes clouded. "It's not the money I'm worried about. You're in too deep, Grace. You can't do this alone. You have to go to the police."

"I can't. Until I figure out who's feeding Kane information, I can't even trust the police." Grace's smile was strained as she glanced at Helen. "You'd better get going before someone sees us together. I don't want to involve you in this mess anymore than I already have."

Reluctantly, Helen stood. "Will you keep in touch?"

"If I can."

"Be careful, Grace. Kane—he's going to be even more dangerous now. As for Rialto and Calderone..." She trailed off with a shudder, her silence more eloquent than words.

LONELINESS welled inside Grace as she watched her friend disappear into the darkness. She was on her own now. There would be no further contact with Helen until Grace and her mother were safely out of the country. Maybe not even then.

Her plan was fairly simple. After the exchange was made, she and her mother would head for New York, to Grace's father's place. Harry Drummond had left them years ago to go chasing after stories halfway round the world, and he'd never looked back. But as successful as he'd become, as arrogant and coldhearted as Grace knew him to still be, she didn't think even he could turn his back on them now. He had the money and clout needed to get them out of the country as quickly as possible, and Grace was prepared to use whatever trickery and coercion necessary to enlist his help.

Once Helen was out of sight, Grace rose with the briefcase and made her way through the café to the street. Outside, she paused, glancing in both directions before she headed toward the parking lot on McKinney.

In spite of the cold, the streets were crowded with the after-work crowd pursuing happy hour with a vengeance in the bars and cafés that lined the West End. Grace didn't pay much attention when someone bumped into her. But when a hand grabbed her elbow, she gasped and tried to jerk away.

"Keep walking," a masculine voice told her. "Don't look back."

Grace's heart thudded against her chest. She had only a split second to decide what to do, but as she gathered her strength to fight back, the man's hand tightened painfully on her arm, as if he'd intuited her response before she had.

"Don't try it," he warned. His voice was low and dangerous, edged with an unfamiliar drawl.

He was too large to be Kane. This man had to be at least six three, with broad, powerful-looking shoulders beneath a sheepskin jacket. Grace was a tall woman, but at five nine, she still had to struggle to match her stride to his.

His face was shadowed by the brim of a Stetson hat, but when she glanced up, she had the immediate impression of chiseled features. Of a strong jaw and a stubborn chin.

"What do you want?" she demanded, trying to cloak her panic behind bravado.

"You know what I want." Almost the exact same words Kane had spoken to her on the phone.

Grace's heart almost stopped. "What makes you think I won't start screaming right here in the middle of the street?"

"That's not your style, is it, Grace?"

The way he said her name...that voice...

Grace stumbled in shock. He hauled her up, grasping her arms in his hands as he steadied her. Their gazes met, and beneath the brim of his hat, gray eyes watched her coldly.

"Brady?" She said his name in wonder, almost afraid to believe it was really him. "What are you doing here?"

"What do you think I'm doing? I came here to protect you." His voice was hard and grim, edged with bitterness as sharp as a knife blade.

"Protect me? But how did you know..." Her voice faded as the impact of the situation hit her. For five years, she'd waited for this moment. Waited for the chance to tell Brady Morgan how sorry she was for what she'd done to him. She had no idea where he'd gone off to when he left the police force, or what he'd been doing all these years. But staring up into his eyes, Grace realized that time hadn't dimmed his feelings for her. He still despised her as much as he had the last time she'd seen him.

"How did you know where to find me?" she finished quietly.

"It doesn't matter. We need to keep on the move. Someone may be following you."

Grace started to glance over her shoulder, but his grip on her tightened. He turned her toward the street and started walking, pulling her along at his side.

"You said you came here to protect me," she said breathlessly, trying to keep up with him. "Who sent you?"

When he didn't answer, she slowed her steps, until he was forced to do the same.

"Who sent you, Brady? Why are you really here?"

"I told you. I'm here to protect you." His voice was as frigid as his gaze.

"What does that mean?" she asked almost angrily.

His jaw tightened. "It means I'm taking you someplace where you'll be safe."

That stopped her cold. She jerked her arm from his grip. "I'm not going anywhere. Not until you tell me exactly what you're up to."

"What's the matter, Grace? Don't you trust me?"

His sarcasm stung, but Grace knew she had it

coming. She lifted her chin. "Right now, I'm not in a position to trust anyone."

"That's why I'm here."

Was it her imagination, or had his voice softened? Hope trembled through Grace, and she closed her eyes briefly. She wanted to believe him. She wanted more than anything to have an ally, but her mother's life was at stake. Brady Morgan had once been an honorable man, but five years could change a person.

So could betrayal.

She gazed up at him, hardening her resolve. "I'm not going anywhere with you. I can't."

"It's not up for discussion. We can do this the easy way or we can do it the hard way. Makes no difference to me."

The insolence in his tone triggered Grace's anger. "Oh, and just what are you going to do when I resist? Grab a fistful of my hair and drag me down the street? Throw me over your shoulder and carry me kicking and screaming into the sunset? Is that the reason for the Marlboro man getup?" Her gaze raked disdainfully over the hat and the sheepskin coat, the boots that made him seem even taller. "Are you trying to convince me you'd actually resort to such tactics?"

He gazed down at her, the gray of his eyes glittering like twin glaciers. "Looks like it's going to be the hard way."

When he reached for her, Grace instinctively flinched away. And at that exact moment, something buzzed by her face. A fraction of a second later, she heard the sound of the gunshot as the bullet crashed into the wall of the building behind her.

The next few moments were a blur. Grace realized she'd been shot at just as Brady lunged toward her. The two of them crashed to the ground, and the air rushed from Grace's lungs. For an instant, the fact that the breath had been knocked out of her frightened her more than the sound of gunshots.

Gunshots. In the plural, her dazed mind finally absorbed. She and Brady were still being fired upon.

Shouts erupted on the street, and the scene became chaotic as frightened onlookers dove for cover. Someone screamed in agony as a stray bullet found a mark. In the pandemonium of thrashing bodies, Brady drew Grace to her feet and all but flung her toward the side of the building.

"Keep low," he shouted as he shoved her roughly toward the alley between the two buildings. He flattened them both against the wall, and with his weapon drawn, he chanced a glance around the corner. A chunk of the building disintegrated over his head, and he grabbed Grace's hand. "Run!"

He didn't have to tell her twice. Grace sprinted up the narrow alley beside him, her long legs pumping full throttle. She wasn't trying to keep up with Brady this time. She was trying to outdistance him if she could. Bullets whizzing overhead could do that.

It wasn't until they'd reached the end of the alley and a padlocked gate barred their way that Grace realized she still clung to the metal briefcase. Brady took it from her hand and tossed it over the fence. Then he easily scaled the mesh, reaching a hand down to pull her up. Her sleeve caught on a wire, and she ripped it loose, scrambling over the fence to land on her feet on the other side.

But Brady collapsed to the ground, clutching his knee and writhing on the ground in agony. "Run!" he gasped. "Keep going."

Sparks flew from the fence as a bullet skimmed the metal. Grace ducked, grabbing Brady's arm. "Come on!"

Flinging off her hand, he fired several rounds into the alley, the sound almost deafening. Grace recoiled, her ears ringing.

"Get up!" she cried. "Let's get out of here."

"Go," Brady said. "I'll catch up."

He fired again as another bullet flashed against the fence. Grace lunged for the briefcase. She wasn't about to leave it behind. The money inside would help her and her mother leave the country. Or at least, it would tide them over until she could contact her father.

She turned back to find Brady struggling to his feet. "I thought I told you to run."

"We're wasting time talking about it." As another round hummed overhead, she grabbed Brady's hand. This time, it was Grace who took the lead.

Chapter Three

By the time they emerged back on the street, sirens wailed in the distance. Behind them, panicked shouts and frightened screams melded with the sirens, the cacophony triggering a battery of memories for Brady, none of them good.

Putting away his gun so as not to frighten onlookers, he limped down the sidewalk next to Grace. He could feel her trembling, from fear more than cold, he was fairly certain, but she probably wouldn't admit it. She'd always been a little too independent for her own good. And a lot too single-minded.

He urged her across Market, using one of the horse-drawn carriages for cover. They moved steadily beside it, keeping the carriage between them and the street. Brady kept hold of Grace's arm, timing their stride to match the gait of the horse. As they neared the parking area where he'd left his rented truck, he pulled Grace into the shadows, glancing over his shoulder. He couldn't see anyone following them, but he knew the shooters were still out there somewhere. He and Grace had to get off the street and fast.

"My truck's just around the corner," he said. "We need to get out of here."

She nodded, too out of breath to reply. If they could make it to the truck, Brady knew he could get them out of here. He hadn't lived in Dallas for nearly five years, but this had once been his town. He knew the back streets and alleys as well as he was coming to know the West Texas terrain. He wasn't sure which turf was more dangerous.

They made a run for it, and after unlocking the truck, he and Grace scrambled inside. Brady started the engine, reversing from the parking space almost before the doors had slammed shut. Within moments, they were merging with traffic on Commerce.

Grace was silent for a change. Brady thought maybe she'd finally accepted the situation—he wasn't leaving here without her—but when the interstate loomed ahead, she sat up and looked around in alarm.

"Pull over."

He shot her a glance. "I don't think so."

"I mean it, Brady, pull over. Let me out."

"Are you crazy? Have you forgotten what just happened back there?"

"We were both shot at. Innocent bystanders were hurt, maybe even killed." Her pale blue eyes looked haunted in the light from the dash. "I haven't forgotten. But I still want out."

"Don't be an idiot—" When he slowed for a traffic light, Grace opened the door. He grabbed her at the last minute, hauling her back in as he swung the truck to the curb. "Are you *trying* to get yourself killed?"

He shoved the gearshift into park as she struggled to free herself from his hold. "Damn it, Grace, calm down. What the hell's the matter with you?"

She looked almost frantic, like a trapped animal trying to get free. "Let me go! I have to get out of here. I can't go with you. I can't leave the city. You don't understand…"

Her voice trailed off, and she glanced away. Her struggles had ceased, but Brady could tell that she would still bolt at the slightest opportunity.

"I understand better than you think. You're willing to risk your life for the sake of a story."

Her eyes glittered, with anger or tears, Brady couldn't tell which. But he assumed it was the former, because he'd never seen Grace cry. Not once.

"You don't know what you're talking about," she said almost desperately.

"Oh, I know. I know better than anyone what you're willing to do for a story." When she tried to jerk free of his hold, his grip on her tightened. "These men are killers, and I'm not just talking about back there. They're brutal and ruthless, and they think nothing of destroying lives. Do you remember the mass graves that were uncovered in Juarez last year? The college students who were mutilated in Matamoros ten years ago because they saw something they shouldn't have? Men like Kane and Rialto did that, Grace, and they have to be stopped. You have the power to put them away, but you won't because it would compromise your precious exclusive.''

He let her go in disgust, but the moment she was set free, she reached for the door handle again. Brady's hand shot out and closed around her wrist, pulling her toward him, and for an instant, their gazes clashed—blue against gray. Her lips trembled, drawing Brady's attention, and a memory whipped through him. He knew the feel of those lips, the taste of them. What they could do to him.

They'd once been so good together, he and Grace, but that had been a long time ago. Too much had gone wrong between them.

But as if to test his resolve, Grace lifted her hand to stroke his cheek, and her lips parted ever so slightly. She moved toward him, slowly, and then her eyes widened in shock as she felt cold metal replace Brady's hand on her right wrist. In one swift movement, he clipped the other cuff to the arm rest.

Grace sat frozen in rage. ''You son of a bitch,'' she finally sputtered. ''This is kidnapping.''

''You think?''

''You can't do this.''

''I just did.'' He glanced in the rearview mirror, then put the truck in gear and pulled back onto the street. Beside him, Grace yanked at the cuffs, her movements frenzied. ''Give it a rest,'' he said gruffly. ''You'll hurt yourself.''

"Like you care."

Her face had gone pale with anger, making the blue of her eyes stand out starkly in the dash lights. Physically, she hadn't changed much, Brady thought. She still wore her brown hair long, letting it curl naturally over her shoulders. The wind had whipped it about, and the tangled strands reminded him of how she used to look waking up in the morning. All that hair spilling down her naked back.

Her legs, still slender and shapely beneath her jeans, stirred even more memories. Grace's legs had always been his downfall.

He tore his gaze away from her and tried to concentrate on the road as he entered the on-ramp of the freeway. Grace didn't utter another word until they were heading west on I–30, toward Fort Worth. She stared sullenly out her window. "Where are you taking me?"

"I told you. Someplace safe."

"Would you care to be a little more specific?"

"Does it matter?"

"Yes, it matters!" She turned in the seat to face him, her expression earnest and desperate, her blue eyes dark with fear. "I can't leave Dallas, Brady. Please. Just take me back. I'll be okay. I know how to take care of myself."

"You still don't get it, do you?" He scowled at the road. "This isn't about you anymore. It's way beyond that. I was sent here to protect you until you can testify against Kane and possibly Rialto, and that's exactly what I intend to do. With or without your cooperation.''

She sat back against the seat, looking drained. ''Who sent you? You're not a cop anymore. What are you? FBI? DEA?''

''Something like that.''

''That's what you've been doing for the last five years? And here I was thinking you'd turned into some kind of cowboy.''

He spared her a brief glance. ''I have.''

She gave a short laugh. ''Brady Morgan, a cowboy? I find that hard to imagine.''

''A lot of things are hard to imagine,'' he said bluntly. ''For instance, after what happened five years ago, I find it hard to believe that you wouldn't be as eager as I am to put Kane away for good. But then, justice was never particularly a concern of yours, was it, Grace?'' He sensed her tension, and almost immediately regretted his harsh words. But sometimes the truth hurt.

''You don't know anything about me,'' she said quietly. ''Not anymore. People change in five years.''

''Don't kid yourself.''

She gave a defeated shrug. ''If you could turn yourself into a cowboy—you, a tough-guy cop who grew up on the streets—why can't you believe I could be redeemed?''

THEY'D LEFT Fort Worth sometime ago, heading in a southwesterly direction on I–30. Traffic thinned once they got out of the city, but a light rain began to fall, and the way the temperature was dropping, Brady was afraid the highway would soon become a mess.

He glanced at Grace. She'd fallen asleep a few minutes earlier, overcome with exhaustion, he suspected. She probably hadn't slept for two days.

He'd been pondering her question for the last several miles, and he thought he knew the answer. Why didn't he believe that she could be redeemed? Simple. Because actions spoke louder than words.

If she truly had changed, she wouldn't think twice about turning over that tape to the police, about giving testimony that would put a ruthless drug dealer behind bars. But she wasn't willing to do that, and so Brady's conclusion was the obvious one. She was still the same conniving reporter she'd been five years ago. She was still willing to sell her soul for the sake of a story.

He'd been well rid of her for the last five years, he thought grimly. Now, if he could just survive the next five days with her....

GRACE HAD no idea how long she'd been dozing, but she would awaken sporadically, shivering with cold. She was finally warm now, almost cozy, and she snuggled deeper into the folds of the blanket.

Not a blanket, she realized groggily. Brady's coat. He'd taken it off and placed it over her, and she wanted to savor that act of kindness. Wanted to believe that he was coming around, but she knew it was wishful thinking. He thought she was refusing to testify because she was holding out for a story. She might have done that once, but not now. She did remember Juarez. She did remember Matamoros. But most of all, she remembered Dallas, five years ago. She wanted to do the right thing, but her mother's life was at stake. Grace could do nothing to jeopardize her mother's safety, not even confide in Brady.

Maybe he could help her, and maybe he couldn't, but what he would most likely do was notify the authorities, whoever he worked for. And then Kane would know she'd talked, and Angeline would be killed. Maybe that would happen, and maybe it wouldn't. But Grace wasn't willing to take any chances, especially since she had no idea who Brady worked for. What she had to do now was get back to Dallas. Anyway possible.

She studied Brady's profile through slitted eyes as she pretended to sleep. A cowboy. Who would have thought it?

His coat smelled of mountain air and wood smoke, and Grace, city-born and raised, was surprised to find that the scent stirred something primal and feminine inside her. She pulled the coat more tightly around her.

He'd removed his hat, too, and she saw that he still wore his hair short, just long enough for a woman's fingers. His jeans were the kind that rode low on his lean waist and fit deceptively snug over long, muscular legs.

When Grace had known Brady five years ago, he'd driven a sports car, in keeping with his undercover image, but he looked at home behind the wheel of the truck. She could suddenly picture him on horseback, looking rugged and sexy. Fiercely masculine.

A cowboy, she thought in wonder. Who would have thought it?

Chapter Four

Brady exited the freeway for gas. When he pulled into the lighted station, Grace sat up and looked around.

"Where are we?"

"Abilene."

Her gaze looked stricken. "That's over a hundred and fifty miles from Dallas. Where on earth are you taking me?"

"Don't worry about it." He opened the truck door, and a blast of frigid air filled the cab. "You may as well relax. We've still got a long way to go."

Grace handed him his coat. "Here, you'll need this. It's freezing outside."

He hesitated, then took the coat, slipping it on as he stepped outside. At the last moment, he glanced back in the truck. "We can get something to eat while we're here. You hungry?"

"Not really." She rattled the handcuffs. "Any chance I could get a potty break?"

Brady hesitated again. He didn't trust her, not for

a second, and his instincts warned him to wait until he'd finished pumping the gas so that he could go into the store with her. But she looked almost pained, and besides, the sooner they could get back on the road, the better he'd feel. Getting out of Dallas had been just a little too easy.

He fished in his jeans pocket for the key, then leaned over and unfastened the cuffs. Grace massaged her wrist as she gave him a wounded look. "I'm not a criminal, you know. You don't have to treat me as if I'm one of your prisoners."

"Then don't give me cause to."

He watched her enter the well-lighted convenience store as he fitted the nozzle into the gas tank. They'd been on the road for nearly three hours, not making very good time. The road conditions were slowing them down. Although he'd seen no indication that they were being followed, he knew Kane and he knew Rialto. Neither man would go down without a fight, and that little shoot-out back in Dallas was just the beginning. They wouldn't let Grace slip away so easily, and Brady wouldn't be at all surprised if Kane's men, maybe even Kane himself, were somewhere on the road behind them.

But there were a lot of ways to leave Dallas, and Kane couldn't have had all the roads watched. It could be that their luck would hold, Brady thought, as he studied the street. It could be that he and Grace would make it to the cabin in the Davis Mountains without further incident.

But he wasn't about to count on it.

THE CONVENIENCE STORE had a sign in the window which proclaimed proudly: Abilene—Where The West Begins. Somehow the slogan deepened Grace's urgency. They were getting farther and farther from Dallas, from her mother, and from the tape that could save her mother's life.

Shoving open the door, Grace walked inside. The store was warm and inviting, with well-stocked shelves of canned food and staples at exorbitant prices. At the end of the counter, a large, plastic cow commemorated the cattle drives that once ended in Abilene.

As Grace made her way to the rest-room area, she resisted the urge to glance over her shoulder to see if Brady was watching her. She knew he was. Watching her like a hawk because he didn't trust her. She could hardly blame him, but to handcuff her like a common criminal. To take her out of Dallas against her will.

Grace realized her anger had more to do with fear for her mother's safety than for what Brady had done. He was trying to save her life, and considering how she'd betrayed him in the past, his actions might even be considered noble. Right now, though, all Grace could think about was getting away from him. Abilene was a fairly large town. There'd be a bus station here, an airport. She could be back in Dallas in a matter of hours.

Inside the bathroom, she took her cell phone from her jacket pocket and checked the battery. She still had a full charge, but it wouldn't last long. She checked her voice mail. Burt had been trying to reach her, but that was it. No number or message from Kane.

What if he wouldn't leave a message? With the phone turned off, Grace would have no way to know he'd called, but what else could she do? Even if she kept the phone turned on, Brady would never allow her to answer it. Better to conserve the battery because her phone might later be her only hope of escape.

Going back out to the store, Grace stayed at the end of the long counter, letting the plastic cow hide her as she glanced outside. Brady was still standing beside the truck, his gaze scouring the street as he filled the gas tank. If she was going to make a break for it, it would have to be now.

"Excuse me," she said to the clerk behind the counter.

The woman was middle-aged, with droopy eyes and a wary expression. "What can I do for you, hon?" A badly chipped front tooth made her lisp slightly.

"This is probably going to sound strange," Grace said nervously, "but is there a back door I could use? I...need to get away from here."

She had the woman's full attention now. Leaving her post by the cash register, she walked over to Grace. "You in some kind of trouble, hon?"

"You could say that. I need to get out of here without being seen."

The woman's gaze fell on the bruise around

Grace's wrist, the torn elbow of her jacket. The dark gaze lifted. "You trying to get away from that hunk you drove up with?" When Grace nodded, the clerk said grimly, "Your old man, huh? I know his type. I been there myself."

"*Is* there a back door?" Grace asked anxiously.

"You bet your sweet ass there is." The woman pointed a bony finger toward the coolers in the back. "There's a door that leads to an alley. You can hide out back there a spell, or you can head on over to Broadway. You might get lucky and find a taxi. You want me to call the cops?"

"No," Grace said, a shade too vehemently. That was the last thing she needed. "I don't want him arrested. I just want to lay low for a while until he cools off, you know?"

The woman nodded. "Yeah, hon, I know."

A FAINT SMELL of decay rose from the shadows in the back of the store, making Grace's stomach lurch. The cooler and storage area were lighted with a bare bulb suspended from a stained ceiling, and Grace could hear the steady *drip-drip* of a leak in the cooling system somewhere nearby.

She found the exit, turned the lock, then drew open the door and stepped out into the frigid mist. Her denim jacket did little to protect her from the cold, and she wished she'd used the credit card she'd stashed in her pocket to purchase a pair of gloves and one of the "End of the Chisholm Trail" sweatshirts she'd seen hanging on a rack near the front of the store. Too late for that now, though. She had only a few seconds before Brady would come looking for her.

Closing the door behind her, Grace scanned the darkness. To her left, she could make out the shape—and smell—of a Dumpster, and in the distance, the glow of lights along the interstate. Grace turned right, but as she stepped away from the door, she saw a figure round the corner of the building and head toward her.

Her heart sank. How had he managed to get around the building so quickly? "I'm going back to Dallas," she said defiantly, as Brady approached her. "Don't try to stop me."

"Get serious, Grace."

"I am serious." She resisted the urge to back away from him. She wasn't frightened of him. This was Brady after all. A man she'd once spent a lot of time with, both in and out of bed. She'd known him back then as well as she'd known herself, or thought she had, but five years had passed. A lifetime of regrets had gone by. People changed, under the circumstances.

He took her arms, and for a moment, they both remained motionless, as if frozen by the icy mist. But his gaze was hot, igniting embers inside Grace that should have been smothered years ago.

Should have been, but weren't.

Okay, she thought resolutely. *So I still find him attractive. I still have feelings for him.*

No good reason why she wouldn't. Their relationship had ended abruptly because of her betrayal. She'd wronged Brady and he'd walked away, leaving her emotions in limbo all these years. But now, suddenly, at the worst possible time, those feelings had come back to life, and her emotions were dredging up some pretty powerful memories.

"After what I did to you, why do you care what happens to me?" Her voice sounded strained, even to her.

His grasp on her arms tightened almost imperceptibly. "It's like I told you earlier. This isn't about you. My assignment is to keep a witness—you—safe until you can testify against Kane. And that's what I intend to do. That's all I intend to do."

His meaning was perfectly clear. She was nothing to him now but an assignment, a distasteful one at that, and although Grace could understand his emotional distance, her pride was still wounded, making her lash out at him. "And if I refuse to testify?"

"You'll be called as a hostile witness. That much is obvious," he said coldly. "But once you're on the stand, I think even you would have second thoughts about lying."

Anger flashed through her like lightning. "I never lied to you, Brady. You can't accuse me of that."

"You may not be a liar, but you're a conniving—"

"Bitch?"

"Don't put words in my mouth, Grace."

"I don't think I have to." Her anger turned to

bitterness. "Your feelings for me are perfectly obvious."

He was silent for a moment, gazing down at her. Grace could barely see his expression in the shadows, but she knew by heart the contours of his face, the gray eyes that could be soft as rain or hard as steel. She knew, without really seeing him, that his lips would be slightly parted as he contemplated their dilemma.

And it was a dilemma, for both of them. Brady had once told her he never wanted to see her again, and yet here he was, duty-bound to protect her. As for Grace—she once would have relished spending time alone with him, having the opportunity to prove to him that she'd changed. But instead, all she could think about was getting away from him. And the hell of it was—she couldn't tell him why. He thought she was after a story. He thought she was still the same hard-nosed, integrity-challenged reporter she'd been five years ago.

Sometimes people grow up, learn from their mistakes, she told him silently. Sometimes people figure out what really matters in this world.

Unfortunately, the revelation had come too late for her and Brady. And if she did manage to get away from him, it would only reinforce for him that he'd been right about her all these years.

Brady's hands slipped down her arms, and a shudder rippled through Grace. His slightest touch had always kindled her deepest passions, and even in the face of danger, she couldn't help responding. He was Brady, after all.

But the moment she felt the cold metal of the handcuffs clamp around her wrist, Grace's desire turned to despair. His gaze darkened on her as he fastened the other cuff around his own wrist. They were joined now, but not in the way she'd wanted.

"How can you do this to me?" she asked desperately. "Take me against my will like this."

"You make it sound like an assault. This isn't personal. I'm trying to protect you."

"I don't need your protection. I can take care of myself." But even as she spoke the words, the sound of the gunshots on Market Street echoed in her head. Kane's words, "If I so much as smell a cop, your mother is a dead woman," reverberated through Grace's being. She was terrified, and if her life had been the only one on the line, she would have welcomed Brady's protection—run flying into his arms, if he'd have her—but she had to think of her mother. Brady couldn't help her save Angeline. Only Grace had the power to do that.

"Do you have any idea who you're up against?" Brady demanded, as if reading her thoughts. "I'm not just talking about Kane, though God knows, he's dangerous enough. I'm talking about Rialto and Calderone. They make Kane look like Santa Claus."

Grace's mind flashed back to the night Kane shot Alec Priestley, his childhood friend, in cold blood, apparently without remorse. That Stephen Rialto and Tomaso Calderone were even more brutal chilled

Grace to the bone, but she knew Brady was right. Kane had murdered quickly, but from everything Grace had read about Calderone and his people, the kill was to be savored.

"Do you remember what happened to those poor DEA agents who were caught by the Calderone cartel in Mexico? They cut out their eyes and gave them to the local witch doctor."

Grace tried to suppress a shudder. Kane was the one she had to worry about now, but if Rialto and Calderone felt threatened by her—

Brady gave a tug on the handcuffs, cutting off her thoughts. "Come on. We need to get back on the road."

Grace opened her mouth to argue, but in her present situation, it seemed ludicrous. All she could do was bide her time. Brady couldn't keep her handcuffed forever, nor could he watch over her twenty-four hours a day. Sooner or later, he would have to sleep. And that's when Grace would make her move.

Without a word, she followed him docilely to the truck.

THE SCENERY changed as Abilene receded in the distance. Timber woods gave way to fenced plains that seemed to go on forever. Through the wet darkness, Brady could make out the silhouette of the oil wells that continued to pump what had once seemed an endless supply of black gold. A lot of the wells had gone dry, but the skeletal remains of the derricks dotting the plains still fed the illusion that all Texans were rich.

Grace was silent, gazing out the window as the miles crept by. She had her head turned from Brady, but he was pretty sure she wasn't asleep. She was over there plotting, trying to figure out how she could get away from him.

What made her so desperate to get back to Dallas? Was getting a story still that important to her?

What else could it be? Brady mused. What other reason would keep her from testifying against Kane and Rialto unless—

Unless she was being threatened.

Was that it? Had either Kane or Rialto gotten to her somehow?

Could Brady have been wrong about her?

Dangerous thinking, where Grace was concerned. He knew all too well what she was capable of, the lengths she would go to for a hot scoop. Instead of trying to justify her motives, he'd do well to keep his mind on his assignment and his eyes on the road.

The interstate was starting to glaze over, and Brady was forced to go even slower. They were inching along the highway, but if Kane and his men were somewhere behind them, the weather would hold them up as well.

Brady had unfastened the handcuffs as soon as they were on the road again, and it was just as well he had. He needed both hands on the wheel, and besides, the forced proximity with Grace had been more unsettling than he cared to admit.

Okay, he thought grimly. She was a damn attractive woman. He'd have to be blind not to see that, and dead not to react to the way her soft, brown hair framed her face, the way her light blue eyes could look right through you. The way her legs seemed to go on forever.

As if sensing his thoughts, she turned from the window to face him. He could feel her blue gaze burning into him, but he kept his own gaze steadfastly on the road.

After a few moments, she said softly, "Why did you quit the police force, Brady?"

He hadn't expected that question. Not yet anyway, but then, Grace had never been one to dance around an issue. He'd once admired that about her. He'd once admired a lot of things about her until he'd had a glimpse of the real Grace.

He shrugged. "You know why I left."

"No, I don't. What happened wasn't your fault."

"The hell it wasn't." He realized suddenly his jaw was clenched, and he worked almost forcibly to relax it. "I left confidential files unsecured in my apartment. I didn't take the necessary precautions when I set up the bust." Brady's failure was still raw, like a wound that hadn't healed properly. He'd walked away from that failure and a career he'd worked years to build, and he'd almost done the same thing after Rachel died. But Mitchell Forbes was not a man you could walk away from that easily. He'd sent Brady back out again, not just to face his failure, but to face his past. He hoped to hell the old man knew what he was doing.

"You had no way of knowing I'd look in those files." Grace's voice was very quiet, almost hushed. "Or that I would listen in on your private phone conversation."

"But I would have known," Brady said bitterly, "If I'd been thinking with my head."

The implication wasn't lost on Grace. He saw her flinch, as if he'd physically struck her. "You still think I went to bed with you to get information."

"Worked like a charm, didn't it? There's a sucker born every minute, as they say."

"Brady..." Whatever she'd been about to say, she never finished it. Instead, she turned to stare out the window again.

After a moment, she said, with her own bitterness, "After that night, you never gave me a chance to explain. You cut me out of your life without a word. You just disappeared."

"What was there to say?" The truck hit an icy spot, and he struggled for a moment to regain control of the wheel. He glanced at her to see if she was frightened, but she seemed unaware of the road conditions. "Look, there's no point in going over this now, okay? It's finished. I've moved on. You've moved on." He shrugged. "Nothing left worth talking about."

"Maybe that's how you feel, but I'd still like the chance to tell my side of things. It's bothered me all these years that I could never explain what really happened that night.''

''We both know what happened.'' Brady frowned at the road. He didn't like rehashing the past. Nothing but a lot of bad memories and some painful regrets back there.

But Grace was insistent. ''I knew you were an undercover narc when I met you, but I swear I didn't get involved with you because of a story. I found out on my own that you were going after Lester Kane, so I started doing some digging. I had a job to do, too, Brady.''

Yeah, and you know what I think of your job. But Brady merely shrugged.

''I could tell from your actions that night that something big was going down. You were—I don't know—wired. Keyed up. When the phone rang, you thought I was in the shower, but I'd forgotten something. I came back into the bedroom. I didn't know where you were, so I picked up the extension. When I heard your voice, I knew I should hang up, but—''

''You didn't.'' His jaw was clenched again, but this time, Brady made no effort to relax. He gave her a cold glance. ''You heard enough to put it all together.''

''Once I'd read the files,'' she admitted. ''The story just sort of unfolded. The biggest drug bust in the city's history was about to go down, and there I was, sitting on the exclusive. I had a way to blow the competition right out of the water.''

''So you wrote the story and got it on the front

page of the *Examiner's* morning edition.'' Brady glanced at her again. ''Only, the bust didn't go down. We were called off at the last minute.''

''I had no way of knowing.'' Grace drew a long breath. ''It was wrong of me to read those files and to listen in on your phone conversation. I admit that. But I didn't print the story, Brady. I wrote it and faxed it over to the paper, but Burt was supposed to sit on it. That piece was never supposed to run until I got your okay.''

''And you think that excuses what you did?'' He gave her an incredulous look and saw her turn away. ''There was no way we could touch Kane after that. He's been out there dealing drugs all these years because—''

''Because of what I did. I know.'' She winced. ''You think that's not the last thing on my mind before I go to sleep at night? I know what I did, Brady. I've had to live with it for the last five years. If there was any way I could go back and change that night, I would. But you can't go back, can you? You can never go back.''

There was a sadness in her tone Brady had never heard from her before, but he knew better than to believe it. ''Okay, so now I know everything. We can just forget it. It's all over and done with.''

''Except for one thing.''

She was gazing down at her hands now, not looking at him. She seemed uncharacteristically subdued for Grace. Remorseful. She lifted her blue gaze and met his. ''It's not over for me, Brady.''

Her words twisted something inside Brady's gut. Some basic instinct told him not to believe her, she was making up the whole thing so he'd let down his guard. But another instinct was telling him something else. To pull the truck off the road and kiss her until the fire that had always been between them erupted like a red-hot volcano.

For a split second, he allowed his gaze to cling to hers, feeling the attraction quiver along his backbone. Grace had one hell of a body, and she knew how to use it. The thought of her in his arms, lying against him, under him. Those long legs wrapped around him....

The tires slipped on the icy pavement, and with a sinking feeling, Brady felt the wheel spin in his hands. They were nearing a bridge, and the truck careened badly, skimming sideways toward the embankment. He tapped the brakes as he tried to steer into the skid.

It didn't work. Gathering speed, they hydroplaned toward the shoulder, but at the last moment, the left front fender grazed the guardrail of the bridge, slowing them. The nose of the truck dipped over the embankment and hung there for one breathless moment before they went crashing down into the gully.

Chapter Five

The truck skidded to a bone-jarring halt at the bottom of a dry ravine. In the shocked aftermath that followed, Grace became aware of two things: the thunder of her heartbeat and an overwhelming regret for having blurted out her true feelings.

Why on earth had she told him? It was true, of course. She never had gotten over Brady, but now was hardly the time to confess unrequited love. Not with murderers hot on their trail and her escape from Brady uppermost in her mind.

Still, she'd waited five long years to tell him how she felt, and a part of her had recognized that it was probably now or never. When she finally did get away from him, it would seem like another betrayal to him. And she wouldn't be able to explain her true motives because she and her mother would be thousands of miles away.

"You okay?" he asked gruffly.

"I'm fine." Her words were as clipped as his.

Obviously, they were both uncomfortable and not because they'd run off the road.

Brady muttered a vicious oath as he pounded the steering wheel with his fist. "Of all the stupid, idiotic—"

"At least the embankment wasn't all that steep," she offered helpfully.

"Yeah, well, this is West Texas after all."

He sounded angry, and Grace wondered if he was mad at himself for losing control of the truck, or at her, for saying what she had.

"Let me see if I can get us out of here." He tried reversing the truck, but the rear tires spun uselessly on the frozen ground. He couldn't go forward, either. "Damn, this is no good." He glanced out the window. "Without any traction, we'll never make it up the embankment."

"Don't you have a cell phone?" Grace asked. "We could call a wrecker." She could feel the weight of her own phone in her jacket pocket, but Brady didn't know about it, and she wanted to keep it that way as long as possible. The phone was her only link to Kane and her mother.

He shrugged. "In case you hadn't noticed, we're stuck in the middle of nowhere. A wrecker could take hours to get out here in this weather." He turned to face her. "You stay put. I'll go see if I can find some rocks or wood, something to wedge under the tires for traction."

Grace reached for her door handle. "I'll help you."

"You're not dressed for this weather." His gaze dipped for one split second to the front of her denim jacket. "I'll leave the heater running. You should be warm enough. I'll try to hurry."

After he was gone, Grace sat shivering inside the truck. The heater was blowing steadily, but her chill had little to do with the cold. The moment the door had closed behind Brady, the idea had come to her that now was her chance to get away from him. She could use her cell phone to call a taxi to come pick her up.

But he'd said it would take hours for a wrecker to get out here in this weather. A taxi probably wouldn't even bother until morning, and there was no way she could hide from Brady for the rest of the night. As desperate as she was to get back to Dallas, she wasn't an idiot. She knew she wouldn't last long in this cold.

The mere thought of spending the night outside in arctic weather made her huddle more deeply inside her jacket. She closed her eyes, thinking about her mother. Wherever Angeline was, was she warm? Were they taking care of her?

Was she afraid?

Tears smarted behind Grace's lids, but she blinked them away. Crying did no good. She'd learned that a long time ago, when her father had walked out on them. Better to keep a cool head and try to figure out what to do.

But the thought of her mother, alone and frightened in some strange place, filled Grace with despair. Angeline was like a child. In some ways, she and Grace had traded places, Angeline becoming the innocent, and Grace becoming the caregiver, the one who worried long into the night. It was up to her now to bring her mother home safely.

Grace wasn't sure how long she'd been sitting alone in the truck when she spotted a faint illumination far down the highway. She watched the glow turn into twin pinpricks of light. A car was coming. A way back to civilization. A way back to Dallas.

She reached for her briefcase in the back seat. The money would come in handy if she had to pay someone to give her a lift.

Shivering with cold, she stood outside the truck, peering through the darkness. She had no idea which direction Brady had gone, or how long he'd be away. If he heard the oncoming vehicle, he might figure out what she had in mind and come running.

Grace hated leaving him alone out here like this, but he had a cell phone and he had a gun. He wasn't without resources, she reminded herself. He'd once been a cop, was still obviously in law enforcement of some kind.

She struggled up the frozen incline, her feet slipping and sliding beneath her. Finally she made it to the top and glanced back at the truck. Brady was still nowhere in sight.

Standing on the side of the road, she watched the lights, but the vastness of the flat landscape made it difficult to judge how far away the vehicle was. Grace started to move closer to the highway, but before she could take a step, Brady grabbed her from behind and spun her around. Startled, she lost her breath. He'd moved so stealthily, she hadn't heard him come up behind her.

"I thought I told you to stay in the truck." His grasp tightened on her arm as he started pulling her toward the slope.

Grace instinctively resisted. "There's a car coming. I wanted to flag it down, ask the driver to take us to the nearest town—"

"But you were going to wait for me, right?" His gaze fell to the briefcase she clutched in her hand. "Thanks, Grace."

"It's not like you're completely stranded," she said lamely. "You have a cell phone."

"Which may or may not work out here." He pulled her toward the embankment. "Come on."

"But we can still flag down the car—"

"Use your head for once," he all but growled. "Someone tried to kill us back in Dallas. The last thing we want is to go waving down strange vehicles in the middle of the night."

When he put it that way—

They were halfway back down the grade when Grace's feet slipped from underneath her. She landed with a thud and slid the rest of the way down the hill on her butt. Brady didn't even bother to help her up. He strode over to the truck and shut off the engine. "Get up. We've got to get moving."

Grace limped along behind him without argument. She couldn't deny they'd been shot at in Dallas, and she knew better than anyone what Kane was capable of. She'd seen him murder in cold blood. Fear for her mother's life had made her think and act irrationally. From here on out, she knew she had to be a lot smarter. She had to get one step ahead of Brady—and Kane—and stay there.

The only cover for miles around was a stand of cedars that grew along the dry creek bed, but Brady headed straight out into the open plain. Their footsteps crunched on the icy stems of last summer's crop as they put distance between themselves and the highway.

The headlights drew nearer, and finally Brady stopped and pulled Grace to the ground. "Lie flat. Don't make a sound or a move."

"But they'll see us out here. There's no cover."

"Haven't you ever heard of hiding in plain sight?"

She'd heard of it, she just didn't put much stock in it.

She lay still just the same. The sound of the car engine grew louder, and Grace held her breath. Beside her, Brady lay tensed and waiting.

When the vehicle passed by, she exhaled in relief, but when she would have lifted her head, Brady's hand on the back of her neck shoved her face ruthlessly to the ground. The frozen stems cut into her skin, and the cold penetrated her thin clothes. No matter how hard she tried, she couldn't control her shivering. But the car had gone on by. They were safe—

Brady's hand was still lodged firmly against the back of her neck when the vehicle stopped fifty feet or so down the road. After a split second, the tires whined on the glassy pavement as the driver reversed.

Other than to hold her down, Brady hadn't moved a muscle. He seemed capable of lying there for hours, if need be. But it was torture for Grace. Not just the cold and discomfort, but the agony of not being able to see what was happening. How had Brady known they were in danger?

Maybe they weren't in danger, Grace thought hopefully. It was possible the driver had glimpsed Brady's truck in the gully and was stopping to help....

Brady's hand was no longer on her neck, but Grace didn't dare move. Up on the highway, the vehicle slithered to a stop, and the doors opened and closed quietly. After a moment, two figures came into Grace's line of view as they crept toward Brady's truck.

When one of them opened the door, she caught a glimpse of his face, and her breath lodged painfully in her throat. It was one of the men who had been in the warehouse the night Priestley was killed. She was almost certain of it.

The truck door closed, extinguishing the light. The men conversed softly to one another, their voices carrying across the open field. They spoke Spanish, too low and rapid for Grace to make out what they were saying. She wanted to turn her head and glance at Brady, but instead she lay perfectly still, her muscles aching from the effort.

Then, without warning, gunfire erupted, and Grace's heart jerked in fear. She thought the men must have spotted them, and her first instinct was to get up and run. But after one terror-stricken moment, she realized they were firing on the empty truck, blowing out the tires and windows with round after round from semi-automatic weapons.

They continued to fire as they backed away from the truck. A bullet struck the gas tank, and Grace heard a loud swooshing sound as a spark ignited the fumes. Seconds later, an explosion rocked the ground like an earthquake as a huge fireball shot skyward.

Grace's hands were in rigid fists pressed against her thighs. She forgot about the cold. The explosion drove everything from her mind but fear. These men were killers. If they saw her and Brady, they wouldn't think twice about turning the weapons on them. Or maybe they wouldn't shoot Grace. Not yet. Not until they had the tape. And men like that had ways of getting what they wanted.

Men like that had kidnapped her mother.

Her heart began to hammer in slow, painful thuds. She had almost flagged them down. She had almost given herself over to them, and worse, she'd almost given them Brady.

She turned her head ever so slightly to make eye contact with Brady, to try and telegraph her gratitude. He was nowhere in sight.

Grace's insides went weak with a nauseating terror. Where was he? He'd been beside her one moment, and the next, he'd vanished as quietly as the falling mist.

Her ears rang in the silent aftermath of the explosion, and the smell of burning rubber stung her eyes. Grace lay shivering on the ground, wondering where Brady was, wondering what she would do if he never came back. Wondering if she would be too late to save her mother. She watched helplessly as the two gunmen separated and circled the stand of cedar trees. It would be only a matter of time before they widened the search, before they spotted her out in the open.

She tasted blood on her tongue and realized she'd bitten her lip. But the pain hardly registered. The rapid thump of her heart made it difficult to think. Grace didn't know what to do. Lie there and wait…or make a run for it.

How much easier her decision would be if she knew where Brady was. If she knew he was okay—

The gunmen disappeared into the cedar thicket, and almost immediately a shot rang out, and then another. Grace half rose in terror. For an eternity, the night seemed to hold a collective breath, and then she saw a shadow emerge from the trees. Brady!

She stood on wobbly legs. The briefcase was still clutched in one hand and as he came up to her, he reached down and took it from her frozen fingers.

"You're okay," she all but whispered. It was a

statement not a question. She reached out and put a trembling hand on his arm, as if to reassure herself. To her amazement—and relief—he didn't push her away. "I thought…when I realized you were gone…"

"It's okay. It's all over." His voice sounded oddly subdued, considering everything that had just happened. He stared down at her for a moment, and though he wasn't touching her back, something passed between them. A silent communication. She'd been afraid for him, and he understood. He'd been afraid for her, too.

"Let's get out of here," he finally said.

Silently, they retraced their steps across the frozen ground. The drizzle had stopped momentarily, and overhead, a few stars twinkled out. In the aftermath of danger, adrenaline rushed through Grace's veins, making her senses seem more keenly alive, the silence more profound. It was strange, but she almost enjoyed the moment—safe now, with Brady beside her.

The smoldering truck loomed in the darkness ahead of them. They stopped and surveyed the damage. "I'm guessing I won't be getting my deposit back on that one," Brady said without much humor.

Grace glanced up at him. "I'd say not. So…what do we do now?"

"We take theirs." He nodded toward the Land Rover parked on the shoulder of the highway.

Grace shuddered, wondering what had happened in the cedar woods but not quite ready to ask.

He said, unexpectedly, "What's in the briefcase, Grace?"

She hesitated. "Nothing important."

"Then you won't mind if I get rid of it." He lifted it as if to toss it into the burning truck, but Grace grabbed for it.

"No, don't!"

"Nothing important, you said." Brady stared down at her in the darkness. "You're not holding out on me, are you, Grace?"

She sighed. "Okay. There's money inside. Ten thousand dollars."

His brows lifted slightly. "Planning to be on the run for a while, were you? Anything else I should know about?"

"The tape isn't in there, if that's what you're getting at."

"Where is it?"

"In Dallas. Take me back, and I'll give it to you."

"Nice try." He opened the briefcase, and a Neiman Marcus shopping bag fell out. He dumped the contents on the ground, and rifled through the money. Then replacing the bills, he handed her the sack. "Better hang onto this. It might come in handy after you testify."

The implication wasn't lost on Grace. Once she testified against Kane and Rialto, she wouldn't be able to go back to her old job, to her old life. She'd end up with nothing except the identity the government created for her.

Brady rose, and before she could stop him, he flung the briefcase into the burning truck.

"Why did you do that?" she asked in surprise.

He glanced down at her in the darkness. "Think about it for a minute. I'm sure you'll figure it out."

He climbed up the embankment without touching her, and Grace was forced to struggle along behind him.

"YOU HAVE TO WONDER how those men found us," Brady mused, almost to himself.

They'd been back on the road for several minutes, hardly saying a word. Grace was still too shaken to speak.

He shot her an enigmatic glance. "You're a smart woman. What's your best guess?"

She shrugged. "We were followed, obviously."

"Lot of ways to leave Dallas. How did Kane know where we were going?"

She hesitated, glancing at him. "You think someone planted a tracking device in my briefcase? Is that why you destroyed it? Why didn't you just search it instead? Then we'd know for sure."

"Because I didn't have time to do a thorough search—take off all the hinges and latches, rip out the lining." He glanced in the rearview mirror, alarming Grace so that she turned to study the road behind them. They seemed to be alone on the highway, but she wasn't sure if that was good or bad.

"Who had access to your briefcase in the last couple of days?"

His question snapped her head back around. "You think someone I know planted the bug?" Her mind flashed to Helen, nudging the case toward her at the café. A little while later, Grace and Brady had been shot at.

But Helen? No way. She was Grace's best friend. If Grace couldn't trust Helen, she couldn't trust anyone. "She wouldn't do that," Grace murmured, almost to herself.

"You mean Helen?"

She glanced at him in surprise. "How did you know I was talking about Helen?"

"Because I saw her bring you the briefcase earlier tonight. How do you think I found you? I followed her from the paper." His gaze went to the rearview mirror again.

This time, Grace refrained from turning around to look at the highway behind them. Instead, she said, "Okay, so if you followed her, someone else could have, too."

"That might explain why we were shot at on Market Street, but not what just happened back there on the highway."

Grace turned to face him. "Assuming a bug was planted, Helen wasn't the only one who had access. The briefcase was in my office. Anyone at the paper could have gotten to it."

"Anyone in particular?"

She hesitated. "I guess I've been wondering about Burt."

"Burt Gordon?" He sounded surprised.

She nodded. "I met him in his office after I escaped from the warehouse that night. I told him everything—about the murder and the tape, everything. He got angry when I wouldn't turn over the tape to him for safekeeping, and he wasn't too thrilled when I called the cops."

Brady glanced at her. "You think he's working for Kane?"

She wrapped her arms around her middle, shivering. "I don't know."

"You surprise me, Grace. I always figured you and Burt Gordon were pretty tight."

"We were. We go back a long way. We started at the paper together. He's given me a lot of breaks, but I can't help remembering that..." She trailed off, glancing out the window.

"Remembering what?"

She sighed. "He's the one who ran that story five years ago after I told him to sit on it. Like you said, the police couldn't touch Kane after that."

Brady was silent for a moment, thinking. "Did he know about your association with Priestley before you went to that warehouse?"

"He knew everything. He's the one who gave me the go ahead to pursue Priestley."

Brady paused again. "Tell me about that night. What happened at the warehouse?"

Grace shrugged. "You already seem to know what happened." Whoever Brady was working for had briefed him thoroughly.

"I'd like to hear it from you."

She drew a long breath and released it. "Priestley wanted me to do an exposé on Kane's alliance with Stephen Rialto and ultimately with the Calderone drug cartel. He wanted out, but Kane wouldn't just let him walk away. He knew too much. He thought if I exposed Kane through the paper, the police would go after him. Kane would be put away, and Priestley would be free of him. But something went wrong. Somehow Kane found out about Priestley. He shot him in cold blood that night. Took out his gun and just blew him away." She said the words almost numbly, but inside, Grace was quivering with fear. That same man, that murderer, had her mother.

"Kane and Priestley were childhood friends," she said. "They went to college together. But when Rialto told him he needed to prove his loyalty so they would know they could trust him, Kane didn't hesitate to pull that trigger."

"You saw Stephen Rialto in the warehouse that night?" Brady asked sharply. "You can place him at the scene of the murder?"

Grace thought back. "I can't be sure it was Rialto. I never got a good look at his face. But the man I saw was definitely in charge. He had authority. And he was accompanied by two bodyguards. I think they were the same men back there on the highway."

Brady muttered an oath as he glanced in his rearview mirror. "I was hoping we were only dealing with Kane at this point, but if those two goons worked for Rialto..." He trailed off, then flashed

Grace a dark glance. "We may be in for a long night."

A shiver of dread traced up Grace's backbone. "I could be mistaken."

"Let's hope you are."

They were silent for a moment, then Brady said, "So, why did Priestley come to you in the first place? Why did he single you out?" His words were quietly spoken, but Grace sensed an edge to the questions.

She answered him just as quietly. "I'd been after Kane for a long time. Ever since you left town."

"Why?"

"I don't think you'd believe me if I told you."

"Oh, I believe you've worked five years to put Kane away," Brady said. "What I'd find hard to swallow is that your motive was altruistic."

"Then don't," Grace said wearily. "You asked me what happened that night and I'm telling you."

"Okay," he conceded. "So what happened after Kane shot Priestley?"

"One of the bodyguards set the warehouse on fire. I had to climb out a window because the door Priestley left open for me was padlocked from the outside. Someone tried to trap me in that warehouse."

Brady didn't say anything for a moment, nor did he look at her. But his profile seemed to harden. He suddenly looked very much like the cop Grace remembered. "Kane was already on to you before that night,'' he finally said. ''You could have been killed.''

''I've taken risks before for my job. Just like you have.''

''You admit you did all this for a story.'' His tone was more grim than Grace could ever remember. It hurt her to hear his bitterness, his utter lack of faith in her.

''That's what you want to believe, isn't it?'' she asked, not without her own rancor.

He lifted a hand from the wheel to massage the back of his neck. ''Why did you call the police from Burt's office? It's pretty obvious you never had any intention of testifying or of turning over that tape.''

''But I did—''

''Then what changed your mind?''

Oh, he was good, Grace thought. Too damned good. He'd put her on the defensive and almost made her blurt out everything. ''I wasn't sure who I could trust. When I got to my apartment, the place had been wrecked. I hadn't told anyone about the tape except Burt and the police. I got scared. Now it seems with good reason.''

Brady watched the road almost fiercely.

After awhile, Grace said, ''Who are you working for, Brady? Don't I have a right to know?''

''It doesn't matter. You know everything you need to know.''

The coolness of his tone sparked Grace's anger. Or maybe it was a release from pent-up fear and tension. ''What do you mean, it doesn't matter? It matters to me. You keep saying this isn't about me. It isn't personal, but it feels pretty damn personal to me. You kidnap me, you take me out of Dallas against my will, you almost get me killed, and it's not personal? I think I at least deserve to know who you're working for.''

''All right, maybe you have a point,'' he allowed, but he hesitated, as if still reluctant to tell her anything. ''It's a specialized branch of the Department of Public Safety.''

''You mean like the Texas Rangers?''

''Not as big. We do a lot of undercover work, so we try to keep a low profile. We've been after Rialto and Calderone for a long time. Kane's involvement is a break. If we get him, we can get to Rialto.''

''That's what I thought, too, and look where it got me,'' Grace said.

''It got you smack-dab in the middle of this thing.'' His gaze met hers for a brief, enigmatic moment before he glanced back at the road. ''We need your help, Grace. We need that tape, and we need your testimony.''

He was offering her a chance to redeem herself. A chance to make things right. Two nights ago, that's what she'd been trying to do. Right what she'd made go so wrong five years ago. But it wasn't that simple anymore. She couldn't turn over the tape to Brady or anyone else until her mother was safe. She couldn't give testimony as long as her mother's life was in jeopardy.

But watching those men destroy Brady's truck

had unleashed a new terror inside Grace. If anything happened to her, who would save her mother? If Grace was dead, Kane would have no reason to let Angeline go and every reason to keep her silent.

Even though her mother sometimes didn't understand what was happening around her, or even who she was, she had her lucid moments, too. Kane wouldn't chance letting her go, and besides, it would be simpler just to get rid of her.

The notion made Grace tremble, and for a moment, the need to tell Brady, to beg for his help was almost overpowering. But could she trust him with her mother's life? Did she have the right?

He was involved in an organization he wouldn't talk about. Moments after he'd found her in Dallas, they'd been shot at, and the gunmen had been able to track them for hundreds of miles. Had her briefcase really been bugged, or had Kane's men had another way of finding them?

Kane had said he had friends in places she couldn't begin to imagine. Did that include Brady's organization?

A terrible doubt stirred. What if both incidents had been staged? What if she'd never really been in danger? What if it was all an elaborate charade to force her cooperation?

Why would Kane want to kill her now? He'd gone to a lot of trouble to kidnap Angeline from the nursing home. He wouldn't have taken such a risk if he hadn't been desperate to get his hands on the evidence Grace possessed. After that, she knew he would have no compunction about killing her and her mother. But until he had the tape…

She glanced at Brady again. His features looked suddenly almost sinister, his demeanor secretive. He was a man Grace had once been halfway in love with, but now he was a stranger.

A stranger she wasn't at all certain she could trust.

Chapter Six

"We'll get off the road for a while. Stretch our legs." Brady glanced at Grace. She hadn't said anything for a long time, and he figured the shock of what had happened earlier was getting to her. Or maybe his questions had made her clam up. He'd hoped her fear would make her open up to him, but instead she'd withdrawn even more. She sat huddled against the door, looking lost and frightened. Alone.

That wasn't the way he remembered Grace. Five years ago, she'd been aggressive, almost arrogant in pursuing what she wanted. She'd been a reporter with an almost overpowering hunger to succeed. Her intensity had sometimes taken his breath away. And so had her passion.

She'd been a woman of extremes, but Brady couldn't ever remember thinking of her as lost and lonely. Certainly not frightened. But she was afraid now. Terrified. And that wasn't like Grace. At least not the woman he'd once known.

She kept insisting she'd changed. Maybe she had.

Maybe he'd been wrong about her. But it was a risk he wasn't willing to take.

"Are you hungry?" he asked her.

She roused a little. "Not really."

"I could use a cup of coffee." He glanced in the rearview mirror. The road behind them was still empty. He needed to pull over somewhere and do some thinking. Figure out how Kane's men—or Rialto's—had found them. "We'll be in Sweetwater soon." When she still didn't respond, he said, "Ever been there?"

Grace shrugged, then said, "Burt tried to get me to cover the Rattlesnake Roundup one year. I declined."

"Smart move." Brady didn't trust the way she was acting. He couldn't be certain if she was trying to lull him into a false sense of security, or if her fear had completely taken the wind out of her sails. "I went with a buddy of mine from college once. His old man hunted rattlesnakes for a living. Western diamondbacks. He'd pump gas vapor down into the holes, then wait for them to come out. Hell of a way to make a living, if you ask me." But then, Brady had hunted his fair share of snakes.

"They use the venom to make snakebite antidotes," Grace said absently.

"And the skin for exotic boots. Some of the local restaurants even have rattlesnake on the menu. Tastes just like chicken."

That got her attention. "You've eaten it?" she asked with a delicate shudder.

"No, but everything tastes like chicken."

She almost smiled at that. "Did your friend's father ever get bitten?"

"Fifty-seven times, he claimed. His system built up an immunity to the poison."

Grace shuddered again. "So, did you catch a rattlesnake?"

Brady grinned. "Nah. But I did get a date with the first runner-up in the Miss Snake Charmer contest."

BRADY'S GRIN had the same effect on Grace she imagined touching a live wire might have. Shock waves rumbled through her, tingling her fingers and toes. Whatever doubts she'd had about him earlier seemed to dissipate. For a moment, she could hardly even breathe.

He pulled into a twenty-four hour truck stop and parked near the back of the lot, where the Land Rover would be well-hidden from the interstate by the eighteen-wheelers.

"Shouldn't we just keep going?" Grace asked worriedly. "What if someone finds your truck?"

"I doubt that'll happen until morning. And even if they do, there's nothing inside that can be traced back to us."

"What about...those two men?" she asked hesitantly.

"Don't worry about them." Without another word, he got out of the Land Rover and Grace did the same. The cold wind was like a slap in the face.

"We've got to pick you up a heavier coat some-where," Brady muttered.

"I'm all right."

"Sure you are. That's why your teeth sound like one of those diamondback rattlers." Almost reluc-tantly, he put his arm around her, drawing her close as they hurried across the parking lot to the restau-rant.

A part of Grace wanted to savor the moment, but another part of her wouldn't allow herself to relax. She wavered between wanting to confide in Brady and not trusting him. She wanted to believe if any-one could help her save her mother, it would be him. But Kane had said no cops, and Grace knew that he was not the kind of man to cross. If he thought Grace had talked to the authorities, he would kill her mother without thinking about it twice.

The restaurant was crowded inside with truckers too weary to battle the deteriorating road conditions. The overall mood was somber as they sat hunched over coffee and sandwiches, contemplating their blown schedules.

With his hand on her back, Brady guided Grace to a booth in the back.

"Just coffee," she told the tired waitress who sauntered over to take their orders.

"Sure you don't want something to eat?" Brady asked her.

"Trust me, I couldn't swallow a bite." She stood. "If you'll excuse me, I think I'll go freshen up." She said it in front of the waitress, so that Brady couldn't stop her without creating a scene, or at the very least, arousing the waitress's curiosity.

But as she walked back to the rest rooms, she could feel his gaze on her. She knew that he would be watching the exit, making sure she didn't somehow slip out.

Not to worry, she thought. The bathroom was windowless, and there was only one way in and out. No escape. She checked her voice mail. Burt was still trying to reach her, even at this hour. She wondered uneasily why he was so desperate to find her. Because Kane had ordered him to?

Reluctantly, Grace punched in the number of Burt's private line at the paper. Even though it was nearly midnight, he answered on the first ring. "Grace? Where are you? What's going on? Are you all right?"

His rushed tone took her slightly aback. But that was Burt. Thin, wiry, he lived on a perpetual caffeine high. She pictured him in his office, jacket tossed aside, shirtsleeves rolled up, suspenders and tie loosened hours ago.

"Why have you been trying to reach me?" she asked cautiously.

"That's a hell of a question!" he exploded. "No one has seen or heard from you in two days. You just up and disappear off the face of the earth, and I'm not supposed to ask where you are? The police are practically camping out here, for God's sake." She heard his chair squeak, and imagined him shifting his sparse frame nervously, his mind splintering in a dozen different directions at once. His voice lowered, ''I've heard Kane's about to be arrested. I need you back here, Grace. This is your story. You can bust it wide open. With that tape—''

Grace's heart started to pound in fear. Kane was going to be arrested? What would happen to her mother?

''How do you know Kane is going to be arrested?''

''I don't actually *know*. It's just a rumor. But the police are acting kind of weird here—''

''Weird how?'' she asked sharply. ''Who have you been talking to?''

Burt paused. ''Are you sure you're okay?''

''I'm fine. Just tell me what's going on there.''

He sighed, and she could picture him running his hand through his thinning brown hair. ''They've got people out looking for you,'' he said grimly. ''It's an all-out manhunt.''

''They who?''

''They, the police. Who else? Listen, Grace. This story is developing hard. It could go national, get you the kind of recognition you've always wanted. Maybe even pit you against your old man for a Pulitzer. Don't tell me you wouldn't get a charge out of that.''

Grace closed her eyes for a moment. It was hard to believe that at one time, the possibility of breaking a national story, of being considered for the same award her father had won twice, had been the only thing that mattered to her. Now it was the least of her concerns.

"Tell me where you are and I'll come meet you," Burt urged. There was something in his voice, an odd, desperate note that frightened Grace. Was Kane holding something over Burt's head, too? "We can talk, figure out the best way to break this thing."

"There's nothing to figure out," Grace said.

Burt's tone was shocked. "What do you mean, there's nothing to figure out? We've got a hell of a lot to talk about. You're an eyewitness to a murder. Some serious players could go down because of that tape you made. What the hell is the matter with you?"

"Tell me something, Burt. Why did you run that story five years ago on Kane when I asked you to hold it for verification?"

"Ancient history, Grace. What difference does it make?"

"I don't know. I've just always wondered what prompted you to risk both our careers to run that story."

"We came out all right, didn't we?"

Somehow Burt had talked his way out of the blame, and he'd managed to keep Grace's job as well. She'd never really known how. "After what we did, Kane shut down his operation for a while. The police had no evidence or witnesses against him. He's been free all these years, dealing drugs, because of what you and I did."

"What's your point, Grace?"

"The point is, I'm not so sure I like what we do anymore. There's not going to be a story from me. I'm not coming back to the *Examiner*. This is good-bye, Burt."

"No! Don't hang up! Tell me where you are! At least tell me where the tape is. Come on, Grace, you owe me. I'm the one who put you on to Kane in the first place, remember? I'm the one who convinced the chief you could handle a story like that. Don't make me sorry for going out on a limb for you. At least give me a chance to listen to that tape before you turn it over to the cops."

Grace hung up without another word. Shivering, she crossed over to the sink and grimaced when she saw her reflection.

"Death warmed over," she muttered, splashing cold water on her face. She finger-combed her hair, then stood restless for a moment, wondering what to do next. Calling Burt had been an impulse, but what had it gotten her? She'd found out that Kane might be arrested, but she still had no idea who had betrayed her, who was on Kane's payroll. She hated not knowing who she could trust. Burt? The police? Helen?

The thought of her own best friend turning against her made Grace feel sick. Made her realize how Brady must have felt all those years ago. No wonder he couldn't forgive her.

In spite of her earlier panic, Grace couldn't bring herself to believe that he was involved in any of this—except as her protector. He'd once been the most honorable man she'd ever known, and back there on the highway, she'd glimpsed something of the old Brady in his eyes. He was sworn to protect her, and he would do so with his life, if necessary. The honor was still there. If she looked closely enough, would she find something else from their past that lingered?

Don't, she warned herself harshly. Brady didn't care about her anymore, and Grace couldn't blame him. She'd killed whatever feelings he'd had for her, and it did no good now to dream about something that could never be again.

AFTER THE WAITRESS had brought their coffee, Brady took out his cell phone and dialed his contact number at the DPS.

"John Kruger," a terse voice answered.

"This is Brady Morgan."

"Agent Morgan, I've been expecting your call. How did everything go in Dallas?"

Brady paused, wondering how much he wanted to say over the phone. The lines were routinely swept, but cell phone calls could easily be intercepted. "We had a few fireworks, but the package is safe."

"And in your possession, I trust."

"Affirmative."

"You're en route to the destination?"

"Affirmative."

"ETA?"

"Hard to say. The roads are pretty bad. We're not making the kind of time I would have hoped for."

Kruger paused. "Has she said anything useful?" His voice sounded forced, as if he, too, were afraid their call might be intercepted. Or as if he had someone in the office with him, Brady thought suddenly. At midnight?

"She hasn't said much. Nothing we didn't already know."

"Maybe you can change that. I understand you and she have a past."

Brady frowned. How had he found *that* out? From Mitchell? Or had Kruger run a background check on Brady? That seemed more likely. Mitchell was extremely reticent about discussing his agents with anyone, including DPS. Brady wondered if that was what Mitchell and Kruger had been arguing about that morning.

"I'll see what I can do," Brady said.

"You do that. Get her to talk, Morgan. Do whatever you have to do, but find out where that tape is."

THE COFFEE was waiting when Grace came back out, and she noticed that Brady hadn't ordered anything to eat, either. The hand that lifted his cup was steady, but there was something in his eyes, a shadow, that made her think about the two men lying back there in the cold.

"You don't have an appetite, either, I see."

He shrugged. "Guess not."

She leaned across the table, lowering her voice. "What happened back there, Brady?"

"You know what happened."

"Those men. They're…dead?"

His gaze lifted to meet hers. Something dark flickered in his eyes. "Not hard to figure that one out, was it, Grace?"

So how does it feel to kill a man? the reporter in her wanted to ask, but the look in his eyes stopped her.

He had the deepest eyes, she thought. Soul deep.

He put down his cup and returned her scrutiny. Neither of them said anything, just watched one another warily while the attraction slowly rekindled. Awareness fluttered in Grace's stomach and quivered along her backbone. Her heart began to beat in long, breathless strokes.

Brady had been an incredible lover. All that intensity. All that dark passion concentrated solely on her.

The way he would kiss her, until she grew weak all over. The way he would touch her, arousing her to the point of desperation. The way he would take her…

She'd almost passed out once, the feelings had been so powerful. Did Brady remember that night? The way he'd held her afterward?

Grace had never experienced anything like it before or since, and she never expected to. Wasn't sure she even wanted to. That kind of frenzy was almost terrifying.

And yet at this moment, with Brady's gaze on her, she felt a shade of that same intensity, a hint of that same passion, and a flush of heat stole over her.

"That was never one of our problems," he said softly.

She didn't need to ask what he meant. The air quivered with electricity.

Grace drew a long breath. "No. We were good together, Brady."

"We were incredible together." His words were grim and resolved. He never took his eyes off her. "Were is the key word."

"I know. It's over."

"For both of us, Grace. It has to be."

She paused, the heat of passion turning into embarrassment. "What I said earlier…about the way I still feel—"

"Forget it. I have."

"Just like that?" He could set her off like no man she'd ever known before. "How convenient to be able to turn off your emotions so easily," she said bitterly.

"You think the last five years have been easy for me?"

"I don't know, Brady. Why don't you tell me?"

"What good would it do?" He leaned across the table, his gray eyes sparking with his own sudden anger. It took a lot to get Brady mad. He'd always had an almost superhuman ability to keep his emotions in check. Except in bed….

"It might help to talk about it—"

"What is it you want to know, Grace? How it felt as if someone had cut out my insides with a rusty knife when I found out what you'd done? Or how about why I really left the force? That's a good one, too. I was forced out. I had no choice. It was leave of my own free will or be suspended indefinitely. I had an exemplary record until then. Did you know that? Is that what you want to hear? How it felt to lose everything I ever cared about in the space of one night? Is that the kind of detail you're looking for, Grace?"

"I'm sorry—"

"It's taken me five years to rebuild my life. I won't let you come along and start picking it apart again."

"I wasn't trying to—"

He stood and threw some bills on the table. "Let's go."

They'd hardly touched their coffee, but somehow Grace didn't think they'd need the caffeine to keep them awake. She had a feeling it would be a very long time before either of them got any rest.

"How long has it been since you slept?"

They'd left the interstate in Sweetwater, following a southerly route which would take them through San Angelo and eventually to I–10, where they would head due west toward the mountains. If they'd stayed on I–30, it would have been a straighter shot—through Big Springs, Midland, Odessa, and finally Pecos. But the smaller roads and highways would be harder to track if someone was following them.

"I figure it's been about forty-eight hours," he said, when Grace responded with a shrug. "Why don't you get in the back seat and stretch out? We've still got a long way to go."

"I won't be able to sleep." But she unfastened her seat belt and climbed over the seat just the same. Her leg brushed against his arm, and it was all Brady could do not to flinch away from her touch. Not because he didn't want it. Back there in the restaurant, he'd discovered something unsettling about himself. After everything Grace had done to him, he still couldn't help wanting her.

But that was the kind of woman she was. Sexy. Ambitious. Dangerous.

The kind that could destroy you, if you let her.

Was that what had gotten him so riled back there? he wondered uneasily. The fact that she still had such a strong effect on him?

Brady could hear her in the back seat, stirring around, trying to get comfortable. He said reluctantly, "Grace, you okay back there?"

A pause, then, "I'm fine."

"Here." He handed her his coat over the seat. "You can use this to cover up with."

"I don't need it. It's warm in here."

"Take it," he said almost gruffly. "You never could sleep without cover."

His words seemed to catch them both by surprise.

She took the coat, and he could imagine her pulling it around her, snuggling deep.

"About what I said…" He trailed off, scowling at the road. "I didn't mean to come down so hard on you."

"Don't worry about it." Her words sounded muffled, as if she had the coat pulled all the way up to her chin. "I understand why you feel the way you do."

"It's just…what happened earlier…back there on the road…"

"I know. I understand."

It was strange, but somehow he thought she did. Taking a life, even a lowlife, wasn't something you walked away from unaffected. He was trying to explain, without really saying the words, that he'd taken his emotions out on her.

He'd done what he had to do. Those men had come after Grace. They would have killed her—or worse—to get what they wanted, and Brady had no qualms about taking them out.

But it still didn't make living with it any easier.

"Brady?"

The way she said his name, soft and tentative, stirred something powerful inside him. "Yeah?"

"Thank you."

"For what?"

"You saved my life. I won't forget it."

"I was just doing my job, Grace." He regretted his harsh words the moment they left his mouth, but he couldn't take them back, and it was probably just as well. This thing between them had to be squelched here and now, before it went any further. He wasn't about to start up again with Grace. He'd learned that lesson.

But as the miles sped by, Brady couldn't stop thinking about her. The farther south they got, the better the road conditions, so his driving no longer required all his attention. His mind was free to wander, and it strayed inevitably to five years ago, when he'd first met Grace.

He hadn't stood a chance. Not with those blue eyes. That long, wavy hair. That body.

But it hadn't been all physical. There'd been something else between them, something immediate and powerful. Something that fueled the passion.

He remembered once taking her to Vegas for a long weekend. They hadn't left their room until it was time to catch the plane back to Dallas, and for three days, Grace hadn't worn anything more than the shirt she'd ripped off him the moment they were alone.

The sex had been great, no question about that. But he'd had great sex with other women. With Grace...

With Grace, it had been all-consuming. Mind-blowing. A little scary even, because he'd never been sure he could handle her fervor.

She said she'd changed now. A part of him couldn't help wondering how much.

THE SKY LIGHTENED behind them, a subtle change at first, and then more boldly as the sun hovered on the eastern horizon. They cruised through the deserted streets of Fort Stockton, still westbound on I–10.

From the back seat, Brady heard sounds of life. In spite of her proclamation earlier that she wouldn't be able to sleep, Grace had been silent for several hours. He figured she'd dozed off sometime before they got to San Angelo.

In the rearview mirror, he saw her sit up and gaze around. Her hair was tangled, her face wiped clean of makeup. She looked vulnerable huddled under his coat. Vulnerable but still sexy.

Their eyes met in the mirror. She quickly glanced away. "Where are we?"

"We just left Fort Stockton. We're still on I–10, heading west."

"Are we almost to our destination?"

"Not long now," was all he said.

They both watched the passing scenery in silence for a few minutes. The plains of Abilene and Sweetwater had given way to more rugged terrain. Mountains with shrouded peaks rose before them, and smoke pluming from a distant chimney was the only sign of civilization for miles. They had the road to themselves.

"There's a place just ahead where we can stop and get some breakfast," Brady said. "The restaurant has a general store next door. I know the owner. She might be persuaded to open up for us so we can get you a decent coat."

"Okay." Grace kept her head turned to the window, and that was the last thing she said until he exited the freeway in Rio Rancho, a tiny ghost town with little more than memories lingering on the ragged streets.

Most of the businesses were boarded up and abandoned, but Leni Crowe—who, in spite of her red hair and blue eyes, claimed to be descended from the Commanches—managed to survive by serving the best *huevos con chirizo* this side of the border.

The restaurant still wore its Closed sign on the door, but there was a light on, and Brady could see movement inside. He banged on the glass door, and after a moment, a shadow appeared on the other side.

"We're closed," a feminine voice informed him impatiently. "Can't you read the sign, moron?"

"Come on, Leni. Open up. It's cold out here."

She paused. "I know that voice. Brady...that you?"

"Yeah. How about taking pity on us?"

"You never were the kind of man to inspire much pity," she grumbled through the glass. But the lock twisted, and she drew back the door. Her gaze went instantly to Grace, and Brady saw the women coolly assessing one another. They were both tall, both striking in their own way. Leni, with her red hair and flashing eyes. Grace, more cool and remote.

"Well, get in here," Leni muttered, stepping back out of their way. "I can't afford to heat the whole damn town. You have any idea what my gas bill runs in the winter?''

She eyed Brady suspiciously once he'd closed the door against the cold. ''So, what are you up to this time, Brady Morgan?'' Her gaze flickered briefly, disdainfully over Grace, then slid back to Brady. ''You're not bringing me trouble, I hope.''

''No trouble,'' Brady said easily. ''We just want some breakfast. You got that grill fired up?''

''It's getting there. You might as well sit down and I'll get you some coffee. I just made it. Black and strong enough to walk out of here on its own two legs, right?''

''The stronger the better,'' Brady agreed. When Leni returned with the pot, he said, ''You still own the general store next door, Leni?''

''Who'd be stupid enough to buy it from me?'' She served Brady first, then poured Grace's coffee. ''What do you need?''

''My friend here needs a warm coat, some gloves, socks, boots. The works.''

Leni spared Grace another brief glance, then shrugged. ''We may have something that'll fit her. She looks pretty scrawny, though. I'll get Luis to start the eggs while we take a look. Go on over. I'll get the key and meet you there.''

''Thanks, Leni.''

''Anything for you, Brady. You know that.''

She flashed him a high-octane smile before turning to disappear into the kitchen.

GRACE STOOD shivering in the cold as they waited for Leni to open the general store. Brady had tried to get her to put on his coat, but she'd stubbornly refused, not really knowing why. It wasn't like he'd get chilled without it. After the look that woman gave him, Grace doubted he'd feel the cold even if he was standing out there stark naked.

An intriguing thought, but she wasn't through with the subject of Leni.

"Who is that awful woman?"

"You mean Leni?"

Grace rolled her eyes. Of course, Leni. Who else would she be talking about? "You two seem to know each other pretty well."

Brady shrugged. "As well as people get to know each other out here, I guess."

"So, who is she?"

"Her name is Leni Crowe. I knew her in college. She used to be married to a cop I knew. After he was killed, Leni moved back out here to live with her father. When he died, she stayed on to run this place."

Grace felt a niggle of guilt for her unkind thoughts. From the sounds of it, Leni had had a hard life. "She must have been pretty young when she lost her husband. I'm surprised she's never remarried."

"She's had a few offers, I hear."

From you? Grace wanted to ask. She was surprised how deeply that notion affected her. Brady...with

Leni. Falling in love with her. Asking her to marry him.

He and Grace had never discussed marriage. They hadn't gotten that far, and besides, both of them had been deeply involved with their careers. The last thing on Grace's mind back then had been marriage. She'd witnessed firsthand how her parents' union had fallen apart, how easily her father had walked away without looking back. No way she'd wanted to put herself through the same, but now, the idea of being married, having someone in her life, someone she loved and trusted, someone she might even want to have children with—

That stopped her short. Not in all her wildest dreams had Grace ever thought of herself as a mother. She'd never considered herself maternal in the least, but after taking care of her mother these last three years, Grace had come to realize that having someone who depended on you, someone who needed you, wasn't a bad thing. In some ways, her life had never been richer.

A light came on inside the store, then the lock turned, and Leni drew back the door. "It's cold in here," she warned. "I turn down the thermostat at night. Saves me a buck or two."

Grace smiled at her. "I don't blame you."

Leni looked almost floored, but she quickly recovered and shrugged indifferently. "Take your time. Stack everything up on the counter over there, and I'll ring you up when you're through."

She busied herself behind the counter, and Grace

glanced around uncertainly. "I guess I need to find a coat."

"You'll need a few spare sets of clothes, too," Brady advised her. "You know best what you need."

He sat down in a chair beside the cash register to chat with Leni, but as Grace walked around the store, examining the clothing, she could feel his gaze on her, making her nervous. Hastily, so as not to leave him alone with Leni for too long, Grace loaded her arms with jeans, cotton turtlenecks, socks, underwear, and finally a black down-filled parka.

"That should do it," she said, dusting her hands. "Oh, wait a second." Quickly, she added a supply of toiletries to the stack. "Now, I'm finished."

She half-expected Brady to protest the size of her purchase, but after Leni had rung them up and given them the bad news, he took out his wallet without a word and paid her in cash.

Outside, Grace tried to thank Brady, but he merely shrugged. "It'll go on the expense account." He took the remaining sacks from her and nodded toward the restaurant. "You go on back inside. I have a little business to attend to."

"With Leni?" The moment the question left her mouth, Grace regretted it. Obviously, whatever was going on between Brady and Leni was none of her business.

She didn't wait for Brady to answer, but turned instead and headed for the restaurant. By the time he rejoined her, their food was ready—steaming plates of scrambled eggs and spicy sausage, refried beans, crisp potatoes, and fresh flour tortillas.

"I'll never be able to eat all this," Grace murmured, eyeing the heaping plate and wondering if she should have gotten her jeans a size larger.

"You might be surprised once you taste it." Brady sampled his eggs, then dashed them with hot sauce.

When he offered her the bottle, Grace shook her head. "No, thanks." The sausage looked spicy enough without adding more heat. Tentatively, she lifted a bite to her mouth and her taste buds exploded. The dish was hot, but Brady was right. She'd never tasted anything so flavorful.

"Wow," she said, her eyes watering. "This is really good, but—" She waved her hand in front of her mouth. "How do you stand it so spicy?"

"It's an acquired taste, I guess." He gave her a sympathetic smile. "Try the beans. You might find them a little more to your liking."

Everything was delicious, but when Grace had eaten all she possibly could and shoved back her plate, she had barely made a dent in the food. Brady, on the other hand, had made a very respectable showing.

As they sat finishing their coffee, Leni came over with the bill. "What'd you think of the Horns this year?" she asked Brady, bending over the table to get their plates. Grace caught a whiff of some potent perfume. *That's funny,* she thought. She hadn't noticed Leni wearing a fragrance earlier. Had she put it on for Brady's benefit?

"They had a pretty good season," Brady said. "I miss the old Southwest Conference, though."

"That Stanley kid's got potential." Leni straightened and smiled down at Brady. "Nothing like you and Danny, though. Those were the days, huh, Brady?"

Brady smiled. "We had some good times."

"The best." Leni seemed reluctant to leave. "Well, I guess I'll see you around, Brady," she said softly.

"See ya, Leni."

Once she'd gone, Grace leaned across the table toward him. "You used to play football for UT?" She and her mother had moved to Dallas when Grace was fifteen, but even a Yankee transplant knew what it meant to play football for the Texas Longhorns.

"Mostly I warmed the bench," he said dryly.

"What position did you play?"

"Quarterback."

That figured, Grace thought. He'd want to be in charge. "Were you any good?"

"I had a decent arm." He shrugged. "Steve Fuller and I were recruited the same year. Ever hear of him?"

"Are you kidding?" Steve Fuller, who still played pro ball, was widely touted as the best quarterback ever to come out of the state of Texas—

which said a lot. "I once interviewed him," Grace said, remembering all that good-old-boy charm.

"Then you know why I warmed the bench most of the time. I was his backup. The guy never missed a game," Brady said without rancor.

"That must have been difficult for you." Brady wasn't the type to relish sitting on the sidelines. In a state where football was almost a religion, it must have been especially hard.

But he seemed more philosophical than embittered. "I was there on a scholarship. Football put me through four years of college. I got an education I wouldn't otherwise have gotten. I did okay."

"Yes, you did," Grace agreed. She couldn't picture Brady playing pro ball, anyway. She couldn't picture him as anything but a cop. "You told me once your mother died when you were twelve. What about your dad? Did he get to see you play football?"

A shutter dropped over Brady's expression. His gaze darkened. "My old man died the same year my mother did."

"I'm sorry. I had no idea." Grace wanted to reach out and touch his hand, make contact with him, but considering everything between them, it didn't seem the right thing to do.

"Nothing to be sorry about." He finished his coffee. "It was his choice."

"His choice? You mean he—"

"Killed himself. That's exactly what I mean."

The words were almost matter-of-factly spoken,

but there was nothing casual about Brady's demeanor. He sat rigid, his jaw like steel. Grace had touched a nerve without meaning to.

"I'm sorry," she said again, not knowing what else to say. "What happened? Unless you don't want to talk about it."

She thought for a moment he wouldn't answer her. He gazed out the window, his gray eyes as bleak as the winter sky, the lines around his mouth as hard and unyielding as the West Texas mountains looming in the distant. "I guess the trouble started in Vietnam. He spent four years as a POW. He came home changed."

"They all did," Grace murmured.

"My mother used to say that he was like a different person. Before, he'd been happy-go-lucky, always wanting people around him. But I never saw that side of him. All I saw was the anger." He paused, still gazing out the window. "He became a cop. I don't think that helped matters. It's a tough job under the best of circumstances. After my mother died, I guess he just couldn't hold it together anymore. He beat up a suspect one night. Put the guy in the hospital. Did some serious damage. After the review board suspended him, he went home in the middle of the day, took out his service revolver, and put a bullet through his brain. End of story."

Brady's gaze finally met Grace's. She was startled by the darkness she saw there. The ghosts. It wasn't the end of the story, she thought. It was only the beginning. Because Brady hadn't told her everything. If his father had committed suicide in the middle of the day, then Brady had probably been at school. He'd probably been the one to come home and find his father's body.

The image burned into Grace's mind. Brady, alone and frightened. Brady, needing someone and having no one.

At least she'd always had Angeline.

"Brady, I'm sorry," she said softly. "I had no idea."

He shrugged. "It doesn't matter anymore. I never talk about this stuff. I don't even know why I told you."

"Maybe because you've needed to tell someone for a long time."

"Don't read more into this than what it is," he said coolly. "We've been on the road a long time. I guess I'm a little punch-drunk."

That was probably true. On the other hand, Grace couldn't help wondering if maybe he'd confided in her because he trusted her a little more than he professed. She couldn't help hoping that was the case.

Chapter Seven

Brady wasn't sure why he'd unloaded all that ancient garbage on Grace, but maybe it had something to do with the fact that he was getting so damned tired he couldn't think straight. Which was a dangerous situation, considering. He'd taken out two men back there on the highway, but that didn't mean Kane and Rialto wouldn't send more. Brady had to be ready for them, which meant sometime in the very near future, he had to get some rest.

But there was still the problem of Grace. He had no doubt she'd bolt at the first opportunity, but what he couldn't figure out was why? What did Kane have on her? It had to be more than just a threat against her life. Grace wasn't the type to run from danger. She was the type to embrace it.

She came to an abrupt halt in front of the restaurant, gazing around. "Where's the Land Rover?"

"I gave it to Leni."

"You *gave* it to Leni?" Grace turned to him incredulously. "Why?"

"Actually, gave isn't exactly the right word. I traded her. For this." He walked over to a dilapidated, red pickup and opened the door, waving Grace inside.

She eyed the truck doubtfully. "You traded her a brand new Land Rover for *this?* Does it even run?"

"Like a scalded dog, knowing Leni. She has a way with engines."

Grace stepped up on the running board and climbed inside, settling herself on the cracked vinyl seat. "Obviously, she's not a bad businesswoman, either," she muttered.

When Brady had gotten behind the wheel and cranked the engine, Grace said, "Aren't you afraid someone will come looking for the Land Rover? Won't that put Leni in danger?"

Brady pulled away from the restaurant without glancing back. "They'll never think to look here, and even if they did, no one will recognize that Land Rover once Leni gets through with it."

Grace wrinkled her nose as she glanced around the ragged truck cab. "You may be right about that," she said, and then they both fell silent as Brady accelerated onto the freeway.

Rio Rancho was soon just a speck behind them. Ahead, weak sunlight glinted off rock, casting a reddish glow on the craggy face of the mountain. As the mist burned away, blue sky peeked from a thick drift of white clouds, but Brady knew better than to hope for a prolonged break in the weather. They were in for more sleet, but once they were safely ensconced in the cabin, the inclement weather could work in their favor.

Grace seemed absorbed in the scenery, although there wasn't much to see. Miles and miles of rocky plains dotted with scrub, mesquite, and cactus. He wondered what she thought of the rugged country. It was a far cry from city life, and even after five years, he still wasn't sure he'd adjusted completely.

Leaving the freeway behind, they turned south again on a two-lane state highway. Grace, reading a road sign, said, "Marfa. I've heard of that town."

"It's where the movie *Giant* was filmed. Elizabeth Taylor, Rock Hudson. Ever see it?"

"I watched it once with my mother. She had a real thing for James Dean."

Brady caught the past tense and said, "Had?"

Grace glanced at him, her gaze shadowed. "My mother hasn't been well. She has Alzheimer's disease."

"That's rough," Brady said with genuine regret. He'd met Grace's mother once. She was a very special woman. "How long has she had it?"

"Three years. Although who knows how long really? She's had memory lapses for years, but nothing we thought was serious. Then three years ago, she started going out shopping and forgetting how to get back home. Sometimes even forgetting who she was. After the diagnosis was made, I persuaded her to move in with me so that I could keep an eye on her. But even though I cut back on my hours at the paper, I couldn't watch her twenty-four hours a day. I still had assignments, interviews, deadlines to meet.'' Grace sighed. ''Six months ago, I had to put her in a nursing home. It's a beautiful facility. Expert care. Private rooms. But it killed me just the same.''

Brady had never seen this side of Grace. He didn't know what to make of her. The woman he'd known five years ago had been ambitious and single-minded to a fault. He couldn't have imagined her cutting back on her hours, turning down choice assignments, putting her career on hold to take care of a sick mother.

It wasn't that he didn't believe her now. He did. He could hear the pain and despair in her voice when she talked about her mother. He could see how deeply she cared. It was just that here was a Grace who was a stranger to him. A woman who could be even more dangerous than the other Grace, and that was the last thing Brady needed.

Her glance seemed hesitant. ''She liked you, you know. She only met you that one time, but she asked about you for a long time afterward.''

Brady smiled. ''I remember thinking when I first met her that she was the most beautiful woman I'd ever seen in my life.''

Grace smiled, too. ''I could tell you were smitten with her,'' she teased.

''Who wouldn't be?''

''She had that effect on everyone she met,'' Grace said. ''She was beautiful inside and out. She still is.'' Her voice broke, and she turned quickly back to the window.

"You're like her in some ways, you know."

She seemed surprised by his words. "I'm not anything like her. I only wish I was."

"You have her looks. You have her passion for life."

She glanced at him reluctantly, her blue gaze brittle. "She would never have done to you what I did."

He shrugged. "We all make mistakes. No one's perfect."

"Are you saying you forgive me?"

He turned back to the road without answering. It was a question he wasn't ready to deal with yet. Once he forgave Grace…once he no longer had her betrayal to use as a defense…

He didn't want to contemplate what might happen. He wouldn't let himself think about the coming days and nights the two of them would spend together in a remote cabin. Cut off from civilization with no one else for miles around.

The nights were cold and lonely in the mountains. How much easier they passed with a warm body to curl up against.

"Does it?" Her voice was soft, but insistent.

Brady rubbed the back of his neck. "I don't know."

Her sigh was heavy. "At least you're honest."

Was he? Was he being honest about his feelings? He'd told Grace it was over between them, but he wasn't so sure anymore.

"Do you live around here?" she asked suddenly, as if wanting to change the subject.

He was more than willing. "Yeah, but we're not going to the ranch."

"You live on a ranch?" She gave him a curious look, a reporter's look. Now that was more like the Grace he knew. "You ride horses, herd cattle, all that kind of stuff?"

"Yeah, as a matter-of-fact." He smiled a little.

"Seriously? I mean, don't they have high-tech equipment to do the hard work these days? Helicopters and three-wheelers for round-ups? I thought cowboys were obsolete."

"Not on this ranch. We do it the old-fashioned way, for the most part."

"Why?" She sat up straighter in the seat. If she was faking her interest, she was a damn good actress.

"Because that's the way Mitchell wants it."

"Mitchell?"

"The owner. It's a thing with him. Keeping the old ways and traditions alive. Ranching is hard work. Grueling work. But it also builds character, teaches you teamwork. Out here—" Brady swept his hand in front of the windshield, encompassing the vastness of the landscape. "You have to learn how to survive in a very basic way."

"I'd like to meet this Mitchell sometime," Grace said softly. "He sounds like a very interesting man."

"He has his moments," Brady agreed.

He turned off the highway again, this time onto a rugged trail that lead straight across the plain toward the foothills of the mountains. As they began to ascend, the road became little more than two rutted-out tracks that ran parallel to a deep canyon carved from the red sandstone mountains. The shadows against the far wall deepened, making the gorge seem bottomless.

The cabin where they were going was a good twenty-five miles from the highway, fifty miles from the nearest town of any size. Brady glanced at Grace's silent profile. She seemed struck by the stark beauty of the landscape, but he wondered if she'd fully absorbed the gravity of the situation. They were literally in the middle of nowhere. No one to rely on but themselves. No one for company but each other.

No one for miles around but the two of them.

THE TRUCK shimmied to a halt beside a cabin that appeared to perch on the very edge of the canyon. Getting out of the truck, Grace scrambled over rocky barriers until she stood on the very rim. Her breath caught at the primitive beauty of the place.

She gazed down into the deep gorge, peering through the shadows toward the bottom. Somewhere in the distance, she could hear the sound of rushing water, but everything else was silent. So quiet she thought they would be able to hear even the slightest noise miles away. The perfect place to hide.

Brady came up beside her. "Pretty bleak out here."

"I think it's beautiful," Grace said breathlessly. She glanced at his profile. Beneath the brim of his hat, the shadow of his beard made him seem as tough and rugged as the landscape around them. He was a part of this country now. He belonged here more than he did in the city, and a part of Grace felt the loss even as another part of her became intrigued by the possibilities.

She turned back to the canyon, staring across the yawning expanse to the boundless vista beyond. The land stretched forever, barren except for a few scattered cactus and agave that managed to survive among the rocks. The air was thin and cold, bone-chilling and yet exhilarating at the same time.

Grace had never breathed air so crisp, witnessed a sky so blue, a landscape so vast. She had the sudden feeling that she was perched on the edge of the world, and that if she were the only one here, it would be the loneliest place imaginable. But with Brady by her side...

"I'd like to write about this place sometime," she said softly.

"What would you write about?" He'd turned to stare at her, and his gray eyes seemed to be searching for something. Grace wasn't sure what.

She shrugged. "You, maybe."

"Not much to interest a reader there," he said dryly.

"You're wrong," Grace said. "A city cop moves

west to become a cowboy. That's a great story. I never even knew you could ride a horse."

He turned back to the canyon, his gaze scanning the distant side in a way that made Grace shiver. You could take a cop out of the city...

"When I was a teenager, one of the big oil companies used to sponsor a bunch of us foster kids to come out to a ranch every summer to keep us off the streets. Teach us the value of hard work. Keep us drug- and gang-free. You've heard the drill."

"Was it the same ranch where you live now?"

"No. It was more like a dude ranch, but I learned how to ride there. Learned to appreciate the land. Wide open spaces. How to live with things I couldn't change." He glanced at her.

"You can learn that in the city, too," she told him. "It might surprise you how much I've learned in the last five years."

"Such as?" His eyes were as deep and shadowed as the canyon before him, his tone faintly challenging.

Grace met his gaze. "I learned what's really important in this world."

"You're talking about your mother."

Fear tingled through her at the mention of her mother. The landscape suddenly turned threatening. Right now, standing on the edge of nothing, it seemed as if a whole world separated Grace from Angeline. "Her illness brought us closer together than we'd ever been. Made me appreciate the things she'd tried to teach me about life. Things like honor and loyalty. Integrity.''

"Pretty words, Grace. Not much more than that, though.''

"You still don't believe I've changed?'' His doubts hurt her more than she wanted to admit.

"Actions speak louder than words. If you'd really changed, you'd do the right thing. You'd turn over that tape, give a statement to the police. Testify against Kane.''

She drew a long breath, expelling it in a cloud of icy vapor. "You don't know what you're asking.''

"You're keeping something from me,'' he said grimly. "I've figured that much out.'' He turned and started walking toward the cabin. "But until you get ready to talk, there's not much I can do to help you.''

"I'm never going to talk,'' she said softly, to herself, but she'd forgotten how easily sound carried out there.

He turned, his gray gaze magnetic. "Never is a long time. Especially out here.''

THE INTERIOR of the cabin wasn't as primitive as the outside. It was actually quite cozy, Grace decided, and under other circumstances, she might have found it romantic, with its rustic cedar paneling and huge, stone fireplace. Indian rugs warmed the plank flooring, and the brown leather furniture looked well-worn and inviting. A tiny kitchen was tucked in one corner, and a pine dining table had been situated in front of a window that looked out on the mountains.

Grace could imagine having meals there—lingering over coffee in the mornings, dining by candlelight in the evenings. Anticipating the night ahead, if Brady was sitting across from her.

He brought in the sacks containing her new clothes and placed them in a room down a narrow corridor. When he came back out, he jerked a thumb over his shoulder. ''That's the bedroom. You may as well get settled in while I start a fire.''

''I suppose indoor plumbing is too much to hope for way out here,'' she murmured.

''Bathroom is just across the hall from the bedroom. There should be plenty of hot water, if you want a shower.''

That was exactly what Grace wanted. She felt as if she'd been living in her clothes for days. My God, she thought almost in surprise. She and Brady had only been together a few hours, but she felt as if she'd gotten to know him better than all the time she'd spent with him years ago. Was it because he'd confided in her things that he never had before? Or was it because, this time, she was more willing to listen?

In the bedroom, she took only a moment to study the sparse, sturdy furnishings, the narrow bed spread with a patchwork quilt, before gathering fresh clothes and moving across the hall to the bathroom.

Brady was right. There was plenty of water and it was hot. Grace lingered under the steam until the water grew lukewarm, and she realized guiltily that the supply wasn't endless.

She dried off, dressed, and by the time she came back out to the living area, Brady had built a roaring fire. Chilled from her still damp hair, Grace crossed the room and warmed her hands over the blaze.

"Nothing like a fire," she said. "Furnaces just don't quite do it for me."

Too late, she realized the implication of what she'd said, the memories her words would provoke. She and Brady propped on pillows in front of the small fireplace in her apartment. Naked and sated, and yet still touching. Still hungry. Still not having had enough of each other....

"I remember how you always liked a fire." His tone was low and intimate, drawing Grace's gaze in spite of herself.

It seemed so strange to her that they were standing here together, after so many years apart, the heat of his gaze warming her as ably as the fire behind them.

Their gazes clung for the longest moment, and then he said, almost roughly, "Judging by how long you were in the shower, I'd say you're still prone to using all the hot water."

"Some habits die hard, I guess." Memories continued to assail her. Brady washing her back, kissing her neck, caressing her skin beneath steaming water until she thought she would die from wanting him.

He took her arms suddenly, startling her. His touch sent a thrill up her backbone, but the hard edge in his eyes made her ask uncertainly, "What are you doing?"

He backed her up, until her legs touched the leather sofa, and she sat down, sinking into the soft cushions. Brady knelt beside her, his gaze never leaving hers. "I'm going in there to take a cold shower," he said. "But first we need to get a few things straight."

"Like what?"

"We're about twenty-five miles from the highway, fifty miles from the nearest town. I'm going to take the truck keys into the bathroom with me, so if you leave the cabin, you'll be on foot. The terrain is rugged to say the least, and if you don't freeze to death before you get to the highway, there's bobcat and javelina to worry about. You know anything about javelina, Grace?"

"It's a wild boar," she said, angered by his tone. "I'm not completely stupid, Brady."

His brow arched ever so slightly. "It's a wild boar with tusks out to here." He measured several inches in the air. "Combine those tusks with a nasty disposition and you've got yourself an animal you don't want to mess with."

"So what you're telling me is that I'm stuck in the cabin," she said coolly. "With you."

"And I'm stuck here with you." His gaze flickered over her, then came back steadfastly to her face. His eyes hardened. "What we've got to do is find a way to make this work. I'm not going to start anything with you, Grace. You get what I'm saying? This is a job to me. Nothing more.''

Her blood turned hot with anger. "I get what you're saying, Brady. Loud and clear. I'll try to refrain from jumping your bones first chance I get,'' she said sarcastically.

His gaze narrowed. "I didn't say that to hurt your feelings. There's still something between us. We both know that. But I'm not going to compromise your safety and my job for a quick roll in the hay. I've learned my lesson.''

"If you're finished, then there's a few things *you* need to get straight." She punched his chest with her finger.

His brow lifted again, as if surprised by the forcefulness of her tone. "Such as?''

"I made a mistake five years ago. I've admitted that. I've regretted what I did to you more than you'll ever know. I've even tried to make up for it. Why do you think I went after Kane?'' she asked angrily. But before he could respond, she continued. "I'm not trying to excuse what I did, but I don't need you throwing it in my face every chance you get, either. You get what I'm saying?''

She could see his own anger working in the gray depths of his eyes, but when he spoke, his tone was almost casual. "Fair enough. We'll let bygones be bygones. A truce?'' He held out his hand.

Grace reluctantly accepted it. "Before you shake my hand, maybe we need to get something else straight. I'm going to find a way back to Dallas, with or without your help."

"That's not going to happen," he said easily. "But just out of curiosity, why do you want to get back there so badly?"

"My mother needs me."

A frown flashed across his features. "Does she…how much does she understand?"

Grace glanced away from his probing gaze. "Sometimes she still recognizes me. Even when she doesn't, she still seems to trust me. I'm all she has. I have to get back to her."

"You wouldn't be any good to her dead. Have you thought of that?"

The bluntness of his words chilled Grace. He always did have a way of cutting to the chase. "Please, Brady."

Her hand started to tremble and his fingers tightened around hers. "Talk to me, Grace."

She wanted to. More than anything.

"I've got people in places you can't begin to imagine."

"I can't," she said softly.

Brady dropped her hand and stood. "I don't know what you're keeping from me," he said, staring down at her. "But I promise you one thing. Sooner or later, I'm going to find out."

THE MOMENT Grace heard the shower running, she headed down the hallway to the bedroom. Removing her cell phone from her jacket pocket, she checked her voice mail. Both Burt and Helen had called that morning, as well as someone from the police department. The last message was badly garbled, but Grace thought she could make out: *Saturday, 6 p.m., Dealey Plaza.*

Was the message from Kane? Was he setting up an exchange for her mother and the tape? Saturday was only two days away. How could she possibly get away from Brady and be back in Dallas by that time?

She would have to find a way. She'd crawl down that mountain if she had to. She'd face bobcat and javelina and whatever other beasts stood between her and her mother. She'd take them all on, even Kane.

But as she turned toward the bedroom door, she realized with a sinking heart that only one obstacle stood in her way at the moment. Brady leaned against the bedroom door, clad only in a pair of jeans, as he glared at her angrily.

Chapter Eight

"Who were you talking to, Grace? Who'd you call?"

He unfolded himself from the door frame and moved toward her in the bedroom. She backed away from him, like an animal trapped by a predator.

"No one."

"You're not as good a liar as I remembered. Or else you're losing your touch."

She shoved back a stray curl almost fiercely. "I told you before—I never lied to you."

"Then why start now?" He'd stalked her across the room, and now she was edged against the bed, with nowhere to run to. She was tall enough so that she only had to tip her head slightly to look him in the eye. Brady had always liked that about her. She was his equal in every way, but right now he had the upper hand, and he was damn well going to keep it that way.

"Let's try this again," he said calmly. "Who were you talking to?"

"I don't owe you any explanations, Brady. This has nothing to do with you."

"The hell it doesn't."

She lifted her chin. "You were sent here to protect me, but I didn't ask for that protection. I don't even want it. So I'm not going to answer to you or anyone else. This is my business."

He grabbed for the phone, but she jerked it away. For a moment, the two of them scuffled like two kids fighting over a toy. When he finally wrested the phone away from her, he checked the display. It was clear. She had fast reflexes. He'd give her that.

He tossed the phone on the bed, then took her by the shoulders almost gently. "What does Kane have on you? What's he threatening you with?"

When she didn't answer, he tightened his grip only slightly. "I could help you if you'd let me."

"The only way you can help me is to take me back to Dallas."

"That's not going to happen. And since you've proven to me that I can't trust you not to get yourself killed—" He released her long enough to whip out the handcuffs from his back pocket.

Her gaze widened. "You wouldn't do that. Not now—"

He flicked them open. "Don't make this any harder than it has to be, Grace."

"I'm supposed to just stand here docilely while you restrain me?" she said bitterly.

"It'd be better if you lie down."

"Don't do this, Brady. Please." Her blue eyes

were soft and pleading, but he knew it was only a momentary lapse. Grace could be hard as nails when she wanted to be. "If I ever meant anything to you—"

"You don't want to go there," he warned her. "Trust me."

He took her wrist and placed the handcuff around it. He expected her to put up one hell of a fight, like she had over the phone, but instead, she lay back on the bed, resting her head against the pillows. He placed a knee on the bed, leaning over her to fasten the other handcuff to the iron railing of the headboard.

A tear eased from the corner of her eye and rolled back into her hair. The sight of it brought Brady up short. "Did I hurt you?"

"What do you think?"

He watched another tear follow the first, and almost against his will, he lifted a finger to wipe it away. "I'm sorry," he said softly. "I didn't mean to hurt you. I'm only doing this because I want to go in and finish my shower, and I can't trust you not to bolt. I meant what I said earlier. It's dangerous out there. You could get seriously hurt on this mountain. I can't allow that to happen."

"No," she whispered. "We can't have you botching an assignment, can we?"

He thought of Rachel, dying in his arms, and her bloodstained face suddenly turned into Grace's. The image was like a knife blade in his gut.

"Why are you looking at me that way?" Grace asked almost breathlessly.

"What way?"

"Like…you care."

God, Brady thought. What a fool he was to ever think this could work. That he and Grace could be alone in a cabin for hours, let alone days, without disaster striking.

Without hormones exploding.

Five years hadn't diminished the chemistry between them. If anything, it was more potent than ever.

She reached up and rubbed the back of her free hand against the stubble on his face. He responded instantly to her touch.

"You look almost sinister, leaning over me like this." Her voice had that husky, intimate quality that had always sent him over the edge.

"I'm not sinister," he managed evenly.

"Yes, you are. You kidnap me, hold me against my will. Handcuff me to the bedpost. And now you look as if you want to—"

"Stop it, Grace."

Her brows lifted. "What?"

"This…verbal foreplay. I know what you're doing, and it won't work."

"Then why are you still in here?"

She had a damn good point. If he had half a brain, he'd move away from her, now, before he remembered the sweetness of her lips, the silkiness of her skin….

Who was he trying to kid? He didn't have to re-member, because he'd never forgotten anything about Grace's lovemaking. The way she kissed. The way she touched him. The way she moved against him.

She'd been like wildfire back then. Blazing hot, out of control, dangerous. And yet there'd been something incredibly feminine about her. Something that had gotten to Brady in a way no woman had ever gotten to him before.

I won't do this, he thought almost angrily, but the moment her lips parted, he knew he was lost. He knew that he was going to kiss her, and he knew, after that, all bets were off.

Her eyes darkened with passion. He felt her hand on the back of his neck, pulling him toward her, and for a split second, Brady tried to fight it. He did. Then, with a groan, he claimed her mouth almost savagely as he lowered himself over her.

Their lips parted, tongues thrusting, tangling, as their hands greedily explored. She was exactly the way he remembered her. Lean and hard and yet incredibly sexy. All woman. Enough to drive him insane.

He twisted his fingers through her hair, never breaking the kiss as he shifted his body more intimately against hers. One hand left her hair to trail down her face, experiencing the silkiness for a brief moment before finding her throat, feeling the lightning quickness of her pulse.

"Brady—"

"Don't say anything," he muttered, shoving up her turtleneck to expose the taut skin of her stomach. He trailed kisses over the flatness as his fingers skimmed the lacy edges of her bra, nudging it aside.

"Brady, no."

That got his attention. He lifted his head, gazing at her through dazed eyes. "No?"

She traced his jawline almost tenderly. "Not like this." She glanced at her handcuffed wrist. "Not like...this."

He couldn't have been stopped more effectively with a bucket of cold water. He almost recoiled from her. Straightening from the bed, he grabbed her cell phone, then turned and strode like a man possessed from the bedroom.

AFTER HE'D SHOWERED and changed clothes, Brady looked in on Grace. He had in mind to apologize to her, but when he stepped into the room, he saw that she was sleeping. Curled on her side, with her hair spilling over the pillow and her lashes shadowing her high cheekbones, she looked like a fragile warrior, strong and yet vulnerable at the same time.

Had she always had that vulnerability? Brady wondered as he unfastened the handcuff from her wrist. Very gently he massaged the skin, feeling guilty for the way he'd treated her, but knowing that he'd had no other choice. If she'd stayed in Dallas, Kane would have eventually found her. He would have killed her, and then he would have had Brady to answer to. But no matter what vengeance he'd sought against Kane, it wouldn't have brought Grace back.

Pulling the quilt over her, Brady stood staring down at her for a moment longer, then he turned and walked quietly from the room.

Placing his gun and his own cell phone on the floor beside him, he stretched out on the sofa, staring at the ceiling. He needed to get a couple of hours sleep before nightfall, but first things first. Picking up the phone, he punched in the number for the secure line to the Smoking Barrel Ranch. Penny picked up on the second ring, sounding slightly out of breath.

"Did I catch you at a bad time?" he asked her.

"No, just the usual chaos," she said cheerfully. "We've been hoping to hear from you. Everything go okay in Dallas?"

"As well as could be expected," he said. The line was secure, but you could never be too careful.

"And your trip?"

"Eventful."

There was a long pause on Penny's end. "Are you okay, Brady?"

"Yeah, I'm fine. We both are. Is Mitchell around?"

"Hold on."

A moment later, Mitchell's gruff voice demanded, "Brady? That you?"

"Yeah, I'm just checking in."

"I heard from Kruger. He said you had the package."

"Safe and sound."

Mitchell paused. "Is she talking?"

"No," Brady said grimly. "And I'm not sure she's going to."

"Well, then you're just going to have to make sure she does. Convince her, Brady. Do whatever you have to."

Did that include seducing her? Brady wondered. Losing his head over a kiss? At least one of them had come to their senses. He only wished it had been him. "I may have been wrong about her," he said. "I don't think she's holding out for a story. I think she's running scared. Kane is threatening her somehow."

"The usual extortion or you think he's got something on her?"

"I don't know. But I want you to have Penny check something out for me. Grace's mother is in a nursing home in the Dallas area. I don't know which one, but have Penny check them all. The woman's name is Angeline Drummond. When you find her, I think we'd better put a guard on her. Round-the-clock protection."

"You think Kane will go after her?"

"If he hasn't already. Grace is more than worried about her mother. She's scared, Mitchell. Terrified of something. Find out what you can and let me know."

"Done," Mitchell said. "What else?"

"We had some trouble on the highway just out-

side Abilene. The local cops may make some kind
of stink about it.''

''We're already on it.''

''Thanks, Mitchell. I'll be in touch.''

''You do that, son. And Brady?'' The older man
paused. ''You be careful, you hear me?''

''Loud and clear.''

Brady replaced the phone on the floor and closed
his eyes, but he couldn't unwind enough to sleep.
He tried to tell himself they were safe here. Hardly
anyone knew where he and Grace were, only Mitchell, Penny, the other Confidential agents. John Kruger.

Kruger was the unknown factor here. Brady
would trust anyone at the Smoking Barrel with his
life—more importantly, with Grace's life—but the
DPS agent was another matter. He didn't know Kruger, and what's more, he hadn't exactly been drawn
to the man. There was something about Kruger's
eyes, the way he talked that had hit a nerve with
Brady. The man was just a little too edgy, not unlike
the way Brady had been as a narc.

That thought should have reassured him, but it
didn't. He'd seen too many cops succumb to the
temptation of an easy buck. They'd been lured to
the other side because sometimes the line between
good and evil was all too thin. Drug trafficking was
the worst because the amount of cash floating
around could be staggering.

Then there was the business of Grace's phone that
still bothered Brady. Had she called someone ear-

lier? Could he trust her not to give away their where-abouts?

Could he trust her, period?

That was the rub, Brady thought. He'd seen for himself that she was a different woman from the one he'd known five years ago. She was softer, gentler, less driven, but she was, nonetheless, keeping something from him.

What Brady had to do was find a way to make her confide in him. He already knew her weakness, but unfortunately, he'd discovered that his own Achilles' heel was every bit as vulnerable as hers.

Don't even think it, Brady warned himself. But he feared the inevitable had been set in motion with that one kiss. Darkness was coming. The long night stretched ahead of them. It was cold on the mountain. Lonely. He and Grace had never been able to keep their hands off each other for very long.

Brady closed his eyes, willing himself to sleep. But the five years he and Grace had been apart suddenly seemed like an eternity.

Chapter Nine

When Grace awakened, she could tell from the shadows in the bedroom that it was late in the day. Discovering that the handcuffs had been removed, she swung her legs off the bed, sitting for a moment as she contemplated her situation.

She was worried sick about her mother. The message on her voice mail earlier had only intensified her fear. *Saturday, 6 p.m., Dealey Plaza.* That the message was from Kane, she had no doubt, but Grace didn't have a clue how she would get away from Brady.

Unless, of course, she simply told him the truth. She could do that, and he would help her without hesitation. She was certain of that. But he might also insist on calling in reinforcements, and that risked Kane finding out that she'd talked. Grace trusted Brady with her life—even with her mother's life— but she didn't trust the organization he worked for. Somehow Kane had been able to follow them out of Dallas, and Grace wasn't altogether convinced her briefcase had been bugged. She wasn't so certain that their whereabouts had been compromised on her end.

Still, if she couldn't find a way back to Dallas on her own, she might eventually have to confide in Brady and pray for the best. She would not, under any circumstances, risk missing the exchange on Saturday with Kane.

Feeling slightly disoriented from her long nap, Grace got up and walked to the bedroom door to peer out. The cabin was so silent, she wondered if Brady had gone out. But then a tantalizing aroma of spices drifted down the corridor, and she realized he was in the kitchen cooking.

Her stomach rumbled loudly as she hurriedly brushed her teeth and ran a quick comb through her hair. Brady glanced up from the stove as she walked into the room, his gaze drifting over her for a moment before he went back to his cooking.

Instantly, Grace remembered the look in his eyes when she'd stopped the kiss. He'd wanted to make love to her, maybe even as much as she'd wanted him to. But not as adversaries. That wasn't the kind of memory she wanted to take with her when she and her mother disappeared.

"Smells great," she murmured as she walked into the tiny kitchen. "Anything I can do to help?"

"No, it's ready. I hope you like chili."

He'd showered and changed clothes after Grace had fallen asleep, but he hadn't bothered to shave. He still looked slightly menacing in spite of his domestic chores. Grace silently watched him as he dished up the chili into ceramic bowls, got out two bottles of Mexican beer from the refrigerator, then carried everything over to the table on a tray.

"This is good," Grace said, digging into the food. "I'm famished."

"Glad to see you've got your appetite back. You're going to need your strength."

"Meaning?"

He took a long swig of his beer, then placed the bottle back on the table. "Meaning you've got a long road ahead of you, Grace. Have you thought about that? After you testify, you're not going to be able to go back to your old life. You realize that, don't you? Even if Kane is put away, there's still Rialto and Calderone to worry about. They're not going to let you walk away from this. It's a matter of pride as much as anything else."

Grace frowned, her appetite suddenly deserting her. She knew she wouldn't be able to go back to her old life, but she wasn't going to embrace the one the government had in mind for her, either. Not unless and until she could make sure her mother was safe, and the only way Grace could do that was for her and Angeline to leave the country. Go somewhere far away, where she didn't have to worry about Kane, Rialto, and Calderone. Where she would never see Brady again.

She glanced out the window where the sun was setting over the mountains. The shadows grew long and distorted in the fading light, making the landscape seem even more bleak and threatening. A loneliness welled inside Grace, deepening her despair until it was like a crushing weight on her shoulders.

"Is Kane threatening your mother?" Brady asked her suddenly.

Grace's gaze flew to his. "Why would you think that?"

"For the obvious reasons." His gray eyes were hooded, but she could see the faint stirring of emotion. Anger? Passion? What did Brady really feel for her? "You're not the kind of person to run from trouble," he said softly. "At least I never thought so."

"I didn't run," Grace pointed out. "You're the one who forced me to leave Dallas."

A shadow of annoyance passed over his features. He said impatiently, "I'm talking about your refusal to turn over that tape. Not agreeing to testify. There must be a damn good reason why you won't do that."

"Maybe I don't want to give up my old life. Have you ever considered that?"

"It's more than that." He shoved aside his half-finished chili. "You're afraid."

When she didn't answer, he reached across the table and took her hand. The action startled Grace, and she flinched. Brady dropped her hand at once. "If he's threatening you or your mother, it's not going to go away, Grace. You know that. You've covered too many kidnapping cases not to know what can happen if you try to handle something like this on your own.''

Grace closed her eyes briefly, the desire to confide in him almost overwhelming. He was right. Kidnappers always told the families of their victims to stay away from the police. Kane's threat was nothing new, except for one thing: he'd somehow found out she'd been in the warehouse that night. He knew about the tape. He knew she'd gone to the police. He seemed to know every move she made, and Grace was very much afraid that if she talked, even to Brady, Kane would somehow find out, and her mother would be the one to pay.

If she didn't talk, if she kept everything to herself and somehow found a way to that meeting with Kane on Saturday, Grace knew that she would be able to get her mother to safety. Kane would come after them, but by that time, they would be out of Dallas. She and Angeline would fly to New York where they would meet her father. With his connections and money, he could help them get out of the country, and then Kane wouldn't be able to touch them.

On the other hand, if she agreed to testify after the exchange was made, it was possible Brady's organization could keep her and her mother safe, but for how long? Once they had Kane, would they still be interested in their witness's welfare, or would Grace end up spending the rest of her life looking over her shoulder?

It was a call she couldn't make yet. She had two

days before the meeting on Saturday. Two days in which she could consider every possibility carefully, weigh all her odds, and hopefully make the right decision in the end.

For now, she would say nothing.

DARKNESS FELL quickly. It was an amazing thing to watch. One moment they were standing on the porch watching a spectacular sunset, and the next thing Grace knew, a dark curtain descended over the landscape. She could barely make out the silhouette of jagged rock against a vast, black velvet sky. Everything had melded into sameness.

But then the stars began to twinkle out, more and more, until the heavens were littered with diamond-bright lights. In her years in the city, Grace had forgotten what a country sky looked like. It was dazzling, breathtaking in its scope, and she scanned the constellations, picking out the Big Dipper and Cassiopeia. A shooting star streaked across the sky, followed by a second, and Grace thought that she had never seen anything so beautiful.

Beside her, Brady said, "You don't get fireworks like that in the city."

"The sky is incredible," Grace breathed. She could understand why Brady had come out to this rugged country, the fascination that held him here. There was a timeless quality to the land, like an ancient masterpiece that had been painted by wind, rain, and time. You could lose yourself out here, Grace thought. Forget why you didn't like to look at yourself in the mirror. "Whose cabin is this, Brady? Yours?"

"No, it belongs to Mitchell."

"Then we must be close to the ranch where you live."

"Close is a relative term out here, Grace. Believe me when I tell you there's no one around for miles."

Grace shivered as they both fell silent.

They stood watching the stars for a long time, but finally the cold drove them back inside. Brady stirred the fire while Grace wandered aimlessly around the cabin. There was no television or radio, and Brady didn't seem anxious for conversation. Grace was at loose ends. She didn't want to talk about her turning over the tape or giving testimony, or why she refused to do either one. But all their conversations seem to lead back to that one topic so after a bit, she excused herself to turn in, even though she wasn't the least bit sleepy.

As she lay in bed, eyes wide open, the night gradually came alive. She heard an owl hooting somewhere nearby and the wind whistling through the canyon. She heard Brady go into the bathroom and the shower start up, and she pictured him there under the steaming water, his body rugged and solid. Waiting for her.

There had been a time when Grace wouldn't have hesitated even a moment to join him in the shower. To let nature take its course. There had been a time when she and Brady couldn't get enough of each other, but a lot had happened in five years. Grace wasn't the same person, and she suspected Brady wasn't, either. The fire they'd shared earlier might only have been a memory, some lingering ember that smoldered but couldn't be fully rekindled.

Did she really believe that? Grace asked herself. Or was her real fear that nothing had changed between them. That the intensity might only have deepened in their five years apart. If that was the case, how in the world would she be able to walk away from him?

Because her mother's safety depended on it, that's how. Grace closed her eyes, trying to draw every ounce of her strength, but tonight, the danger seemed so far away. And Brady was so close…so very close…

The bathroom door opened and shut, and she heard his soft footfalls in the hallway. Had he paused in front of her door? She held her breath, but after a moment, she heard the clatter of dishes in the kitchen. He was fixing himself a cup of the strong coffee he loved, bracing himself for the long night ahead.

Grace stared at the ceiling and sighed.

A SOUND awakened her. She thought it was the wind at first, moaning through the canyon, but then she recognized Brady's voice and Grace shot up in bed. He was talking to someone in the other room. His tone was low and urgent, almost pleading. She'd never heard Brady sound that way before.

Getting out of bed, Grace padded on bare feet to

open the bedroom door a crack. Brady's voice grew stronger, insistent. "Don't die on me, you hear? I won't let you die!"

Grace's heart slammed against her ribcage. She realized almost at once he was having a nightmare, and she felt as if she were eavesdropping on something very private and intimate. She didn't know what to do. Go back to bed and pretend she hadn't heard him? Let him sleep on in that agony?

She couldn't do that. He was in terrible pain, and Grace couldn't stand to hear it. She opened the door and headed down the corridor. He lay on the sofa in front of the fireplace. The fire had died down in the night, and Grace stood shivering in a T-shirt.

"Come on, breathe!" he said urgently.

Was he dreaming about his father? Grace wondered. Was that the memory that tortured him?

She crossed over to the couch and knelt beside him. His head thrashed on the pillow. He was covered with a quilt, but he'd pushed it away, exposing his bare chest and shoulders. Tentatively, she placed her hand on his chest, feeling the hardness of his muscles, remembering the strength of him.

Her touch seemed to calm him. He fell silent, and his breathing evened. Grace stood and moved to the fireplace, stirring the embers, then throwing on another log. Once she had the fire going, she turned back to Brady. He was awake and watching her.

Her heart jerked painfully, and a thrill of awareness shot through her. She wondered suddenly if he had anything on underneath the quilt.

As if reading her mind, he threw off the cover and swung his legs over the side of the sofa. He wore jeans, but nothing else, and firelight flickered over the hollow of his chest, the thick, corded muscles in his arms. He ran a hand through his hair as he gazed at her skeptically. "Couldn't sleep?"

He seemed unaware of his nightmare. Grace shrugged. "It was getting cold in the cabin. The fire almost went out."

"Sorry." He got up to stoke the already raging blaze. "I must have dozed off for a while."

"You're entitled. It was a long night last night."

"I'm not being paid to sleep," he muttered, replacing the iron poker on a hook at the side of fireplace. He glanced at his watch. "It's still a few hours till daylight. Why don't you try to go back to sleep?"

"I'm not tired," she said without thinking. He was probably trying to get rid of her, but like an obstinate child, she wasn't cooperating. She sat down on the hearth, letting the fire heat her back through the T-shirt. "I had a long nap when we got here, remember? I don't need anymore sleep."

"Good for you." He sat down on the floor and leaned his back against the sofa. Stretching out his long legs, he crossed his feet and stared into the fire.

"Can I ask you something, Brady?"

He lifted his gaze to hers. Firelight flickered deep inside his gray eyes.

"It's...personal," she said.

He shrugged. "You can always ask."

Meaning he might not answer. Grace hesitated. "You were the one who found your father's body, weren't you?"

The only emotion he showed was a slight tightening of his mouth. "That's a little morbid for this time of night. Besides, what difference does it make?"

"I've been doing some thinking," she said softly. "You said your father was suspended before he...died. When you were faced with a suspension, you left the force. You disappeared. I'm wondering if there's a connection."

"You're into pop psychology now, Grace?"

She gave him a wry smile. "I've had some practice. It might surprise you to learn that I see a therapist from time to time. You're not the only one with unresolved issues, Brady."

He lifted a brow at that. "Unresolved issues? That's way too deep for three o'clock in the morning." He folded his arms across his chest as he returned his gaze to the fire. "The only unresolved issue I have at the moment is keeping you safe until you can testify."

"Liar."

He scowled at her tone. "Give it a rest, Grace."

She watched him watch the fire. He studiously avoided her gaze, and Grace thought that she had hit upon something he'd worked very hard to conceal. His father's death had affected him deeply. Scarred him, because it had opened a door that could never completely be sealed again.

"Do you know who my father is?" She slid off the hearth, and drew up her legs, resting her chin on her knees.

"You told me once he's some hotshot reporter for one of the networks."

"Harry Drummond. Ever hear of him?"

He met her gaze in surprise. "Harry Drummond is your father? *The* Harry Drummond?"

Grace nodded. Her father had first made a name for himself as a young foreign correspondent covering the Vietnam War. He'd been sent to Southeast Asia when Grace was just a baby, and even though he'd come back to the States for a while after the war, he hadn't come back home. He'd gotten himself a new apartment, moved in a girlfriend, but rather than divorcing Grace's mother, he simply pretended his wife and daughter didn't exist.

"He left my mother and me when I was just a kid," she said with a frown. "He never sent me birthday cards or Christmas presents, just a check every month without even so much as a note. It was like I didn't exist to him, except as some financial responsibility he couldn't quite bring himself to shirk. My mother used to watch him on the news every night. Even after everything he did to her, she would still get this light in her eyes when he came on the screen. She would tell me all about the exotic countries he visited, the exciting stories he reported. She made him sound like some kind of hero. I grew up wanting to be exactly like him."

Grace stopped for a moment, glancing at Brady.

She didn't want him to think she was making an excuse for what she'd done in the past. It wasn't that. She wanted him to know that she had some understanding of how his father's death had affected him, changed him.

"When I was a teenager, I started wondering why he never called or wrote, why he never came to see me. It became almost an obsession with me. So one night, I took the subway uptown, found his apartment, and somehow got the courage to knock on his door."

"Don't tell me," Brady said, his dark eyes shadowed by the flickering firelight. "He wasn't home."

"Oh, he was home all right. He had company, a new girlfriend, I guess. A model. He didn't even recognize me when he opened the door. He thought I was just some delivery girl or something, and he tried to shoo me away."

"I'm Grace," she told him. "Your daughter?"

The man in the doorway stared at her for a moment, his brows drawing together as if he'd been confronted with a pesky problem he had little patience for. He was a handsome man, but Grace had known that. What she hadn't known about—what the camera expertly disguised—was the coldness in his eyes, the almost cruel set of his mouth. "What do you want?" he asked her brusquely. "Money? I don't have much cash on me." He turned from the door as if to get his wallet, but Grace caught his arm.

"I don't want money. Did you hear what I said? I'm your daughter."

"And you expect me to do what? Celebrate?" He folded his arms over his bathrobe, sighing heavily. *"Look, I don't know what Angeline has told you about me, but the two of us struck a bargain a long time ago. I agreed to support you financially until you're twenty-one, but that's all. I don't want to hear about your problems. I don't want to know about your life. I'm not the fatherly type. You shouldn't have come here."*

Grace swallowed back painful tears as she glared at him, unable to comprehend that someone could be so cruel. *"But you are a father. My father."*

"I never wanted to be. I never asked to be." He must have realized then how he sounded, and some remnant of decency made him add, *"Look, I'm sorry, okay? That's just the way it is. I never wanted the responsibility of kids. Angeline knew that."*

"You left her because of me?" Grace whispered, the shock of his words vibrating to her very soul.

"Go back home," he said almost angrily. *"Go back to your mother. God knows she was willing to give up everything for you."*

He'd gone back inside and closed the door in her face, and Grace had only seen him in person one time since then. She'd attended the Press Club dinner in Washington several years ago with a prominent *New York Times* reporter. She'd literally bumped into her father, and he'd smiled at her pleasantly enough as he steadied her, but he hadn't recognized her. There hadn't been so much as a glimmer of familiarity in his eyes, and that had hurt Grace even more than the confrontation outside his apartment. She had vowed then that she would make something of her life. She would become a reporter every bit Harry Drummond's equal. She would make him recognize her, make him acknowledge her, and then she would make him sorry for not wanting her.

She shuddered, remembering what she'd been willing to do, who she'd been willing to hurt to accomplish that goal.

"I guess what I'm trying to say is that I understand how deeply we can be hurt by our parents. How their actions can affect us even after we're adults and should know better."

Brady gazed at her warily. "Why are you telling me all this?"

She gave a brief shrug. "I don't know. Maybe because you opened up to me yesterday morning. You told me something about yourself I never knew before. I wish we'd talked like this five years ago. Maybe it would have changed things for us."

"As I recall, we didn't do much talking, period."

Excitement fluttered in her stomach as their gazes met. Grace knew what he meant. Back then, their passion had done the talking for them. Conversation had taken a back seat to more primal needs, but she realized now what a mistake that had been. Brady was a man worth getting to know in every way.

The passion was still there. The need was still as

strong as ever, but it was tempered now with reason. Responsibility. Reality.

"I've done a lot of thinking since you left." Grace lifted a hand to tuck a strand of hair behind her ear. "I'm not trying to make excuses for what I did, but I understand now why I did it. What drove me to it. I wanted my father's attention. His respect. I was willing to do whatever it took to get it. Even betray the only man I ever really cared about."

"Grace—"

"I know." She smiled at him in the firelight. "It's over. You're not going to start up with me again, and I don't blame you. This isn't an ideal time for me, either," she said ironically. "But who knows what tomorrow holds? I'd like you to know—I'd like for you to believe—that I've grown up. I have my priorities straight. I hope someday you can forgive me for what I did to you."

He glanced away from her then, staring deep into the fire. But Grace couldn't tear her gaze away from him. He was so ruggedly handsome, probably the best-looking man she'd ever known, but it wasn't just his appearance that held her awestruck. It was the man inside. Dependable and steady, and yet mysterious. A man of passion. A man not without his own demons.

"I haven't been completely honest with you," he said finally. "I told you I left the force because I was facing a suspension. That was true. I took the easy way out, just like my old man did. But it wasn't just the prospect of losing my career that made me run. I didn't want to face you.''

Grace's heart started to thud. ''You didn't want to face *me*? Why? You hadn't done anything wrong.''

He shrugged. ''I was afraid that after everything that had happened, after everything I'd lost, if I saw you again, if I touched you...'' He trailed off as his gaze lifted to meet hers. ''I'd still want you.''

Grace was having a hard time breathing now. She could only stare back at him. ''But...why?''

''Because you hurt me. More than I ever thought possible. I didn't want to take that kind of risk again. So I did what my old man did. I checked out.''

''If only I'd known you felt that way.''

''What would you have done?'' His dark gaze challenged her. ''Used all your investigative know-how to find me? I didn't want to be found.''

Grace had a hard time fighting back tears. So many years wasted, and now it was too late. Because of what she'd seen in that warehouse, there would be no future for her and Brady. No second chances. Nothing but a lifetime of regrets.

He seemed to realize that, too. He said wearily, ''Go to bed, Grace. There's no point in looking back. What's done is done.''

She swallowed painfully. ''I know that. But it breaks my heart to think how you must have hated me all these years.''

''I never hated you.'' He closed his eyes for a moment, as if fighting his own emotions. ''But God knows I tried.''

Chapter Ten

It was time for the sun to come up, but a gray haze covered the horizon. Brady had been chopping wood for several minutes, but he paused now to catch his breath as his gaze scoured the mountain. The temperature had dropped sometime before dawn, and a fine mist fell like an icy curtain over the dreary landscape.

He was in a foul mood this morning, but he wasn't sure if his temperament was affected by the weather or by the conversation he'd had with Grace. By the revelations they'd made to one another.

He didn't know why he'd let her draw him into a conversation like that. He didn't like talking about himself or his feelings. He wasn't sure why he'd opened up to Grace the way he had, but one thing he did know. No good could come of it. They were stuck together in this cabin by necessity, but that didn't mean they had to get all chummy and cozy. Emotional distance was imperative in his line of work, and with Grace, that distance was even more crucial. She'd made him lose his head once, and he'd lost his self-respect in the process. Brady wouldn't let that happen again.

He wouldn't let history repeat itself, in more ways than one. He had a job to do here, and he couldn't afford to let emotions, hormones, or anything else get in his way. He'd lost one witness. He would not lose another.

At the thought of Rachel, a coldness seeped through him. If he'd protected her as he should have, if he'd kept her alive as he'd promised her, she would have testified against Stephen Rialto. She would have put him away for good, and there would have been no alliance with Lester Kane. Grace might not be in the danger she was in today if Brady had done his job.

He didn't believe in making the same mistakes twice.

He wouldn't.

He picked up the ax, and with renewed vigor, swung it toward the chunk of wood. The blade sank deep, and the wood split cleanly in two. Brady tossed both pieces toward the pile he'd started at the back of the cabin, then picked up another. The physical activity felt good after the hours he'd spent on the road and in the cabin.

After a while, his muscles twitched from the strain. He knew he would pay for the exertion later, but so much the better. Maybe the discomfort would keep him from thinking about Grace.

But as he caught a glimpse of her in the cabin

window, staring out at him, he felt a sinking feeling in his stomach. Chopping wood for a solid week wouldn't get her out of his system. Out of his head.

There was only one way to do that.

HE'D TAKEN OFF his coat, and beneath the cotton shirt he wore, Grace could see the strain of his muscles as he drew back the ax, then swung it downward. She'd been watching him for several minutes, but every time the blade connected with the wood, she still jumped. The power in his arms and back was a sight to behold. She felt exhilarated and excited thinking of all that strength and remembering the tenderness. The way he had held her at times as if she were made of porcelain.

She still remembered the way he'd whispered her name, his voice husky and deep with emotion, his breath warm against her ear, his hands stroking her until her skin flamed wherever he touched.

He was right. They hadn't done much talking back then. But they had communicated. They'd known instinctively what the other needed. When to be passionate and when to be gentle. When to hold and when to let go. They'd both been fiercely independent, and yet after Brady had left, Grace had come to hate being alone. She'd turned to her mother, and that had been a blessing. She and Angeline had grown closer than they ever had been before, and Grace wondered now if that would have happened whether or not she and Brady had been apart. She hadn't been mature enough to nurture both relationships, and so maybe it was best things had turned out they way they had. Maybe things did happen for a reason. Her mother had needed her, still needed her, more so now than ever, and Grace couldn't let anything—even her feelings for Brady—jeopardize her mother's life.

Tearing her gaze away from Brady, she scanned the mountainside. They were a long way from civilization. She couldn't walk out of here in this weather, over this terrain, but Brady kept the truck key with him. He'd even taken her cell phone. Grace could see no recourse but to tell him the truth. Beg him to keep silent until she could make the exchange with Kane.

She trusted Brady, but if he contacted his superiors, would they make Angeline a priority, or would she become an indispensable pawn in their quest to get Kane?

A flash of light up on the mountain caught Grace's attention, and she stared at the spot for a moment, wondering what it was. Reflected sunlight was her first thought, but the sun wasn't shining. The day was damp and cold, and she shivered, even though the cabin was warm inside.

She saw the flash again, and in the instant she realized what it was, the report of a rifle echoed down the mountain. Out of the corner of her eye, she saw Brady drop to the ground, but it was only a glimpse because she'd already turned toward the door, screaming his name.

The wind seemed to rip the knob right out of her

hand as she jerked open the door. There was only a front entrance to the cabin. Brady was around back. Grace plunged through the icy mist toward him, coming to her senses at the last minute. At the corner of the house, she knelt, peering around it.

Another shot rang out, and a chunk of the cabin splintered, piercing Grace's skin with tiny, wooden missiles. The pain barely registered. She'd caught a glimpse of Brady, and he was still on the ground. Not moving.

"He's okay," she whispered. He had to be. She reminded herself of the way he'd lain so still and silent in the field by the highway. He was simply making sure the shooter didn't have an easy target. Grace knew she had to do the same.

She knelt at the corner of the house, out of sight, as her heart pounded inside her. "Brady?"

"Get back inside, Grace."

Thank God, he was alive. Grace rested her head against the cabin for a moment, weak with relief. "Are you okay?"

A slight hesitation, then he said harshly, "Get back inside. *Now!*"

His voice sounded strained, ragged. As if he were in pain.

Grace's pulse hammered in her throat. He'd been hit. She was certain of it. But how badly, she had no way of knowing.

She glanced around the corner of the cabin again. She saw him lying behind the woodpile. He'd pulled himself up to lean against the wood as he peered up the mountain. His weapon was drawn, but what sent shock waves vibrating through Grace was the blood on his shirt. It was all over him, and she felt her stomach tremble in fear.

She started toward him, keeping low. Another shot rang out, the bullet whizzing over her head to become lost somewhere over the canyon. But instead of retreating back to the cabin, Grace dove toward the woodpile.

''I thought I told you—'' Brady's slurred words broke off as his head lolled back against the wood. He was about to pass out, and Grace knew that if he lost consciousness, she would never be able to get him inside.

She pulled him toward her, cradling his head in her arms. ''Brady! Come on! Stay with me. We have to get inside.''

''Get to safety....''

''We'll both get to safety. Come on. I'll help you. Just don't die on me, okay? Don't you dare die on me!''

Grace knew she was babbling, but the sound of her voice kept her steady. She put her hands under Brady's arms and tried to lift him, but his weight was too much for her. ''Come on, help me!'' she cried.

He tried to shove her away. Digging in his pocket, he pulled out the truck key and placed it in her hand, closing his fingers over hers. ''Take the truck. Don't look back.''

Grace opened her hand and stared at the key. A

wave of dizziness came over her. This was what she'd been waiting for. A chance to escape. A way back to Dallas. Brady was giving it to her. Risking his life to save hers.

Her mother needed her. Kane would kill her if Grace didn't get back in time.

But Brady might die if she left him here.

She stuffed the key in her jeans pocket and grabbed him again. "We're both getting out of here. Come on, Brady. Don't bail on me here. We've come too far."

"...always were stubborn as hell," he muttered, rousing enough to allow her to pull him to his feet.

She draped his arm over her shoulder, and when he leaned heavily against her, they both almost toppled back to the ground. But setting her jaw, Grace willed herself to move one foot at a time as she supported Brady's weight.

They made it to the corner of the cabin, and both of them leaned heavily against it, catching their breath. "The shooting has stopped," she murmured.

"They're moving in," Brady rasped. "We've got to get out of here."

Leaving their belongings inside the cabin, they headed for the truck parked in front of the cabin. Grace helped Brady inside, and then she ran around and got in on the driver's side. Her hands were sticky with his blood, and for a moment, panic seized her.

Brady slumped in the seat beside her, his head thrown back. His face was white and drawn with pain, his shirt drenched with blood. She had to get him to a doctor and fast, but first, they had to get off this godforsaken mountain.

She started the engine, and said a silent thanks to Leni when the motor turned over on the first try. Brady had backed the truck into the drive by the cabin for just such a getaway, and Grace jerked the gearshift into drive while simultaneously stepping on the gas. The truck shot forward so quickly she almost lost control. For a moment, they hovered precariously at the edge of the canyon before Grace whipped the wheel to the left, frantically guiding the truck into the narrow ruts that served as a road.

Brady groaned, clutching his arm. Grace knew he had to be in agony, and the bumpy trail hardly helped matters. It was all she could do to keep the tires in the ruts. The rocky face of the mountain rose to the left of them, and to the right, the canyon fell away into nothingness. It occurred to Grace that if their pursuers somehow had gotten ahead of them and blocked the road, there would be no way to turn around. They would be trapped.

Brady had told her they were twenty-five miles from the highway. The condition of the road kept their pace at a crawl, and to make matters worse, the mist froze on the windshield. Grace took one hand off the wheel long enough to turn on the defroster full blast, but the glass fogged badly. She wiped a hand across her window, trying to clear a porthole. In the side mirror, she glimpsed a movement behind them. She checked the rearview mirror, hoping she'd imagined the motion.

But something was behind them, coming up fast. In the instant Grace recognized the vehicle as a four-wheeler, another one seemed to leap off the side of the mountain onto the trail. And then another.

Her heart slammed like a torpedo into her ribcage. On the highway, the truck could have outdistanced the four-wheelers without a problem, but on the rocky trail, the all-terrain vehicles had the advantage. They didn't have to stay in the ruts, but took to the center in between, flying along the jagged road as though it were a racetrack.

The drivers wore visored helmets that protected their faces from the wind and rain. As one of them drew nearer, Grace glimpsed a rifle in his hand. With practiced ease, he lifted the weapon without slowing, and Grace instinctively ducked a split second before the back glass exploded.

She thought Brady had passed out, but the sound of shattering glass, or perhaps the gush of icy wind, roused him. He glanced out the back glass, grimacing.

"Damn!" He drew his own weapon. "Watch out," he shouted. "He's moving up on your side. Try to cut him off."

Grace glanced in the outside mirror. The ATV had pulled even with the truck, trying to get position to fire into the cab. Grace whipped the wheel to the left, letting the bed of the truck fishtail out of the ruts. The bumper missed the four-wheeler, but not by much. His speed slacked for a moment before he punched the gas, and the vehicle reared on its back tires.

He came racing after them again, but before he could draw even, Brady took aim out the window and fired. Grace braced herself for the shot, but the sound sent a shock wave through her just the same. Struggling with the wheel, she had only a brief glimpse of the driver pitching backward, and then slumping forward as the four-wheeler raced off the road and slammed into a boulder.

The other two drivers opened throttle, and the vehicles sprang forward. As they approached the back of the truck, they separated, one coming up on the driver's side, the other hugging precariously close to the canyon.

Brady maneuvered his gun through the shattered window and fired again, but the four-wheelers kept coming.

"Cut the wheel to the right," he shouted.

"I'm afraid I'll lose control," Grace yelled back. And if she did, they'd plunge off the road into the gulch. They'd never survive.

"Cut him off!" Brady ordered.

When Grace hesitated, he reached over and yanked the wheel toward him. The truck careened violently toward the canyon, the wheels slipping on the wet trail. Grace felt a jolt as the truck collided against the four-wheeler. She thought she heard a scream as she glimpsed the vehicle and driver disappear into the abyss. Her heart in her throat, she watched helplessly as the nose of the truck skidded toward the edge. One moment she was braced to go flying into nothingness, and the next, she was fighting the wheel, tapping the brake, somehow coaxing the heavy truck back into the ruts.

The third ATV roared along beside her, trying to urge her toward the edge. Grace kept her position, but the vehicle gained on her. He raised his gun and fired, and Grace's first thought was that he'd missed. There was no sound of breaking glass, no scream of pain from either her or Brady. But then, as the truck pitched badly, she realized with a sinking heart that the driver hadn't been firing at them. He was firing at the tires. And he'd hit at least one.

"Keep going!" Brady opened his door and climbed out, balancing himself on the running board. Then he swung himself over the side and into the back. At the same time, the ATV driver dove for the truck. Grace caught only glimpses of the struggle in the back because it took all her attention to keep the truck on the road.

She heard a gunshot, screamed, and as she glanced in the mirror, she saw a body fly from the back of the truck. Her heart pounding in terror, she forced her eyes back to the road and saw in horror that they were heading for the edge of the canyon. The flat tire gave her no control. She was powerless to stop the momentum.

She heard Brady scream, "Jump!" as the truck took a nosedive into the gorge.

Chapter Eleven

Brady stared in horror as the truck went over the canyon. For a moment, he stood paralyzed, hearing the crash of metal against rock, and then finally, a mile below, the explosion.

"Grace." Her name was hardly more than a whisper on his lips as he limped toward the canyon. The brutal cold tore through his shirt, ripping his arm with pain, but he welcomed the ache. It would keep him conscious long enough to get to Grace.

He didn't question that he would get to her. He'd climb down the face of the canyon wall. He'd do whatever he had to to get to her, but what he couldn't know, what it killed him to contemplate, was the condition in which he would find her.

"Grace." He whispered her name again as he stood at the edge of the gorge, staring down. Then louder, more desperate, "Grace! Grace!" Her name echoed off the canyon walls. Brady thought he'd never heard a sound so forlorn. So final.

Then, miraculously, he caught a glimpse of movement about ten feet below him. A ledge jutted out from the rocky wall, and as Brady stared at the spot, he saw the movement again. Then he heard her moan.

Unmindful of his own wound, he scrambled down the canyon, grabbing at the scrub brush that grew between the rocks. He reached the ledge and knelt awkwardly beside her. She lay on her back, and when she saw him leaning over her, she started.

"It's okay," he soothed. "You're going to be all right."

A cut on her forehead oozed blood, but it didn't look too deep. What worried Brady the most was the possibility of broken bones. If Grace was seriously hurt, he had no idea how he would get her out of there.

She struggled to sit up, but he eased her back down. "Let's check you out first, make sure nothing's broken."

"I'm okay," she mumbled dazedly. "I jumped out of the truck."

"Thank God you did." As gently as he could, he ran his hands over her arms and legs. "All right," he said, when he could detect nothing broken. "Let's see if you can sit up."

She did so with a groan, tentatively moving her arms and legs, her neck. She glanced up the face of the canyon. "How do we get back up there?"

"Same way I got down. We climb." Brady helped her to her feet. "Use the scrub brush and rocks for hand- and footholds,'' he instructed. ''Just take it slow and easy. I'll be right behind you.''

She did as he said, using her height to propel her from one hold to another. Her foot slipped once, and an avalanche of dirt and gravel showered Brady, almost making him lose his grip. Grace glanced down in a alarm. ''Are you okay?''

''Just keep going,'' he said through gritted teeth. His arm had gone from searing pain to icy numbness. He didn't think that was a good sign.

Grace scrambled over the edge and reached a hand down for him. He accepted it gratefully. He hauled himself up, and the two of them collapsed on the icy trail. Brady closed his eyes and stars swam in blackness. He could hear Grace's voice, but she seemed a long way off. He couldn't get to her. He couldn't protect her. She was too far away.

A part of him knew he was losing consciousness even as another part of him welcomed the velvety warmth of the darkness. He tried to call Grace's name, but he couldn't form the word. He lay drifting in that endless void, unable to tell her that he forgave her.

That he loved her.

HE CAME TO slowly. His first awareness was of pain. A sharp, tearing sensation in his left arm that sent a wave of nausea rolling through him. He noticed the cold then, and realized he was shivering beneath a thick blanket. The chill was bone-deep, and for a moment, he wished he hadn't awakened. The darkness had been warm, and the pain had been nothing more than a distant throb. He had to grit his teeth now to keep from passing out again.

Slowly, he opened his eyes. Shadows danced across the ceiling and walls of the room in which he lay, and somewhere nearby, a light flickered. There was warmth nearby also. Instinctively, he moved closer, turning his head to gaze at the fire.

He wasn't in a room, he realized suddenly, but in a cave. He could feel the cold rock beneath him, but he had no idea how he'd gotten there. Struggling to sit up, he gazed around. Grace was lying on the other side of the fire. She'd been sleeping, but the moment she heard him stir, she shot up, her eyes wide and frightened.

"It's just me," he said softly.

He held his arm, trying to assuage the pain, and Grace scrambled around the fire to kneel beside him. "Are you all right? How does your arm feel?"

"Like hell," he admitted, grimacing. "What happened?"

"You were shot back at the cabin."

He had only a vague recollection of the morning's events. Their location had been compromised. They'd been pursued by the gunmen. Leni's truck had gone over the canyon. He'd thought Grace was dead.

He glanced at her sharply. "Are you okay?"

"I'm fine. Just a few cuts and bruises." When he tried to touch the cut on her head, she flinched away. "I said I'm fine."

"Okay." He put up his hand in acquiescence. "It only seemed fair that I take care of you after what you've done for me."

"I didn't do much." She drew her legs up, hugging her knees by the fire. "There wasn't much I could do."

He glanced around the cave. "How did we get here?"

"I stumbled across it." She gave a slight shrug. "I was looking for wood to build a fire, and I found this place. At least we're out of the wind and cold in here."

"But how did we *get* here?" Brady asked, watching her. Firelight flickered in her blue eyes, making her seem almost mystical.

She gave him an ironic smile. "It wasn't easy. You weren't very cooperative."

He had a hazy memory of struggling over rocky terrain, supported by Grace, who at times must have had to almost drag him.

Then once she'd gotten him inside the cave, she'd gathered enough wood to start a fire. He let his gaze linger on the blaze for a moment, awestruck in spite of himself at her ingenuity.

"You're a regular Girl Scout," he murmured. "What'd you do, rub two sticks together?"

"Not quite." He saw her shudder in the firelight. "There were matches in the dead man's pocket. I also took his coat."

Brady glanced down at the parka that had been thrown over him. He remembered now that both he and Grace had left their coats at the cabin. He'd taken his off while chopping wood, and she hadn't been wearing hers when she came out to see about him. They hadn't had time to do anything after that but dash for the truck and make a run for it.

She'd been wearing a long-sleeve shirt over a turtleneck, he remembered. Now she wore only the turtleneck. He glanced down at his arm, noticing for the first time the blue cotton bandage.

"I cleaned it as best I could," she said softly. "There's a stream nearby. I washed away the blood, but I didn't have anything to use as disinfectant. We need to get you to a doctor, Brady."

He lay back, memories drifting over him. A terrible pain in his arm. Grace poised over him, her face white. A knife in her hand.

"Did you cut out the bullet?" he asked weakly. He turned his head to stare at her.

Her eyes widened. "What?"

"You had a knife—"

She let out a breathless laugh. "I thought you were out of it. I didn't think you'd remember. I didn't cut out a bullet. I used the knife to cut away your sleeve. The bullet just nicked your arm. It's only a flesh wound, as they say in Westerns, but it looks pretty nasty. I'm serious about that. We have to get you to a doctor."

He stared at the shadows flickering over the rocky roof of their shelter. They had more pressing concerns than finding a doctor. The safe house had been compromised, and only a handful of people knew of its location. The road wasn't even shown on any maps. The assailants must have used a trail through the mountain to get into position. They'd waited until Brady had come outside before they'd started shooting, which meant they hadn't wanted to storm the cabin. They hadn't wanted to risk hitting Grace until they had that tape.

"Did you call anyone on your cell phone yesterday?" he asked suddenly. "Did you give anyone our location?"

"No." She frowned down at him. "How could I? I don't even know how to explain where we are."

"Someone obviously found out somehow."

"Not from me." She hugged her legs tighter to her. "I didn't talk to anyone."

"But you were going to. You had your cell phone out."

"I was checking my messages." Her tone sounded defensive, and Brady realized again that she was keeping something from him.

"This is important, Grace. We could have been killed. Now isn't the time to hold out on me."

"I'm not!"

"You haven't spoken to anyone since we left Dallas?"

Anger flashed over her features, but she hesitated, giving herself away. "Okay. I talked to Burt when we were in Sweetwater. But I didn't tell him anything."

"Why did you call Burt? I thought you didn't trust him."

"I don't. But he'd been trying to call me, and I thought he might know something." She shrugged helplessly. "Look, I didn't tell him where we were or where we were going. I didn't even know. However those men found out about the cabin—it didn't come from me. What about you?" She glanced back, her gaze challenging. "Have you talked to anyone since we left Dallas?"

He'd talked to John Kruger on the road, and then at the cabin, he'd called the ranch and spoken to Penny and Mitchell. They both knew where the cabin was located, as did the other Confidential agents. But he wouldn't believe anyone at the Smoking Barrel had betrayed him. He couldn't. They were his family now.

He glanced up and found Grace's gaze on him. She said softly, "The leak must be on your end, Brady. You realize that, don't you?"

He sat up, his hand unconsciously going to the throb in his arm. "We don't know where the leak is at this point. Cell phones can be monitored—"

"I didn't call anyone from the cabin. My cell phone couldn't have been monitored." She looked at him almost pityingly. "What about this Mitchell you told me about? Does he know about the cabin?"

Brady glanced away. She wasn't saying anything that hadn't passed through his own mind, but hearing it put into words made him feel disloyal to a man who had found him at one of the lowest points of his life, taken him in, given him a second chance, but even more importantly, had given him a sense of belonging—a feeling Brady hadn't known since his mother died.

Mitchell Forbes would never betray any of his agents, but what of the others? Jake, who was like a brother to Brady. Rafe, who could charm birds out of the sky, but would fight to the death for a cause he believed in. Or for a friend. And Cody, the youngest of the group, but a man Brady wouldn't hesitate to have watching his back. Penny Archer was something of an enigma, Brady had to admit. He didn't know all that much about her background, but he'd always found her to be highly competent and intelligent. Loyal to a fault, although at times he'd sensed a faint resentment in her at being stuck in the office while the agents flew off to various assignments. But would that resentment lead her to betrayal? Brady was hard-pressed to believe it.

That only left John Kruger. The Confidential agents operated on a need-to-know basis only, but as the point man for this assignment, the DPS agent could have been briefed by Mitchell on the location of the safe house. He could have been the one to leak their whereabouts to Kane, maybe even to Rialto, but why?

The obvious answer, of course, was money. He wouldn't be the first agent to change sides in the war against drugs.

"Brady?" Grace was staring at him worriedly. "Are you okay?"

"Just thinking."

"About the leak?"

He shrugged. "We can sit here all day speculating who sold us out, but the fact is, at the moment, it doesn't much matter. We can't stay in this cave. We'll freeze to death when night comes, and besides, we don't have any food. We've got to find a way to get out of here."

Grace pointed toward the coat Brady had discarded. "I think his four-wheeler may still run. It hit a rock when the driver jumped onto the truck, but it doesn't look too badly damaged. Maybe we can use it to get to the highway."

Brady nodded. "I'll go check it out. Just sit tight until I get back."

"But—" She scrambled to her feet when he got up. "You shouldn't be out in the cold. Your arm—"

"You said yourself, it's just a nick. I admit, it hurts like hell, but we can't stay here, Grace. You know that."

"I'll come help you then."

"We've only got one coat."

"But—"

He took her shoulders, ignoring the white-hot pain that shot up his arm at the movement. "You've done enough, okay?" He smiled down at her, allowing himself to touch her face tenderly. "You saved my life. Let me take over for a while."

"Male chauvinist," she muttered, but her mouth softened at his touch. Her eyes glistened. He wanted more than anything to kiss her at that moment, but he only had so much strength left. Time enough for that later.

"I'll be back as fast as I can."

"Brady?"

He turned at the cave entrance. Backlit by the fire, she looked almost angelic, standing there. Something stirred inside Brady, a longing he hadn't known in a very long time. Not since he'd left Grace.

"Be careful," she said softly.

"Always." Then he turned and stepped out into the frigid weather.

GRACE SAT huddled by the fire, watching the cave entrance. Brady had been gone a long time. Hours, it seemed, and she was worried. She'd used the last of the wood she'd gathered earlier, and though the cave was fairly warm for now, the fire would eventually burn itself out and the cold would come seeping in.

What if Brady was hurt? What if he'd passed out from pain? What if he'd been ambushed?

Grace put her hands to her face, imagining all sorts of horrors. Finally, unable to stand the torment any longer, she got up and moved to the opening of the cave. The moment she left the fire, the cold invaded her thin clothing, and she stood shivering as her gaze scanned the desolate countryside.

The sky had changed during the day, the steely morning gray morphing into an eerie greenish black. Storm clouds rolled in from Mexico, and lightning flashed over the canyon. Thunder rumbled through the cave, and Grace wrapped her arms around herself, wishing Brady would hurry back.

The lightning, though still distant, was like nothing she'd ever witnessed. Jagged slashes of fire, one right after the other. It was as mesmerizing as it was terrifying, and Grace watched the storm for a moment before retreating back into the cave. She saw at once that the fire was almost gone, and she glanced back at the opening. She had no idea when Brady would get back. If he didn't come soon, she would freeze to death. She had to get more wood before the rain started.

Without a coat, she had nothing to protect her from the cold, and as she hurried out into the storm, Grace had never felt so vulnerable. The lightning moved closer, and her heart raced even harder. As she stumbled over the rocky terrain, a new terror filled her. Darkness had come early because of the storm. What if she couldn't find her way back to the cave?

She'd been gathering wood beneath a rocky ledge that jutted out about six feet above her. As Grace turned to make her way back to the cave, she heard a noise somewhere above her, a low, feral growl that sent a chill up and down her spine.

Backing away, she scanned the darkness. On the precipice above her, amber eyes watched her. Terror slicked through her. She tried to remember everything she'd ever read about wild animals. Make no sudden moves. Don't let them sense your fear.

A flash of lightning gave her a glimpse of tawny

fur, a smallish head. A mountain lion, she thought. A large one.

She heard the growl again, and then the cat moved to the edge of the parapet. For the longest time, he stared down at her, not crouching, but alert and menacing just the same.

Something hung over the ledge, and Grace thought it might be the remains of a small animal. If the mountain lion had just fed, he might not attack. But then, in another flicker of lightning, she recognized what lay on the ledge with the huge cat. A human arm. The fingers were curled into a fist.

A wave of horror rolled over Grace, and she said on a gasp, ''Brady!''

''Don't move,'' he said behind her.

Relief made her legs go weak. ''What do we do?'' she whispered.

''Start backing slowly toward my voice. No sudden moves.''

She still carried the firewood in her arms, and Grace clutched the pieces like a lifeline. Her gaze never leaving the mountain lion, she inched backward, in the direction from which Brady had spoken.

After a moment, she felt his hands on her arms, steadying her. From the ledge, the huge cat continued to watch them.

''Keep moving,'' Brady said. He took a stick of wood from her arms and slowly raised it over his head. The mountain lion eyed him for a moment, then padded to the other side of the ledge, settling down again with its kill.

When they were about thirty feet from the precipice, Brady said, "Turn and walk as fast as you can back to the cave."

Grace did as she was told. She glanced back once to see if he was following her, and their gazes met in a flash of lightning. "Keep moving," he said.

Once they were safely back in the cave, Grace let the wood tumble from her trembling arms. She leaned back weakly against the rocky wall. "I thought…oh, God." She tried to catch her breath. "There was an arm on that ledge, Brady."

He nodded, his expression grim. "One of the men on the ATVs. The cat must have gotten to him pretty fast."

"Is that why it didn't attack me?"

"Maybe. Cougars are usually pretty elusive. It's uncommon to even see one, and they're nocturnal. The scent of blood must have drawn him out of his lair."

Grace shivered, remembering the sight of that arm. The fact that the man, when he'd been alive, had tried to kill her and Brady didn't lessen the horror.

"What took you so long to get back?" she finally managed to ask.

"I got the four-wheeler going, so I rode back to the cabin to pick up some supplies."

For the first time, Grace noticed the stack of items on the cave floor. She recognized her coat, and realized suddenly that part of her chill was from cold and not fear. Drawing on the parka, she warmed her hands over the dying fire. "Should I put on more wood?"

Brady walked over and picked up the rest of the supplies. "We're leaving. You up for a long ride?"

"On a four-wheeler?"

"Unless you want to walk out of here. Bundle up," he advised. He handed her the items in his hand. "It's going to get cold out there."

It was already freezing outside, but Grace didn't point out that fact. Wordlessly, she pulled on the thick gloves and wrapped a wool scarf around her neck. Brady had retrieved his coat, too, and his hands were encased in a sturdy pair of cowhide gloves, his head protected by the Stetson. He looked tall and solid, wearing that hat. A little dangerous.

He handed Grace a helmet. "Put this on."

She took it reluctantly. "What about you?"

"I'll be okay. Let's head out. The sooner we get started, the sooner we get to where we're going."

"Where are we going, Brady?"

He shrugged. "At the moment, I'm damned if I know."

Chapter Twelve

The cold bit through Brady's sheepskin coat, making the wound in his arm throb. A couple of times, on the way back to the cabin, he'd almost passed out, but he'd held on to consciousness by sheer force of will. He'd do it now, too. He'd get them off this damn mountain if it was the last thing he did.

Maybe it would have been smart to hole up in the cave until morning, but he didn't know how many men might be out looking for them by now. He had no idea how their location had been compromised, but one thing was certain. He wasn't taking any chances. From here on out, he and Grace were on their own. He wouldn't even call Mitchell, and the fact that he could no longer trust a man who had been almost a father to him didn't sit well with Brady. Mitchell wasn't the leak. Brady couldn't believe anyone at the Smoking Barrel Ranch would turn against him, but then, he once would never have thought Grace capable of betrayal, either.

Even through the heavy coat, he could feel her arms around him, holding on tightly as the ATV sprinted over the rocky turf. They were on the trail, making good time, but not good enough. Brady resisted the urge to open throttle because the headlight had been broken when the four-wheeler smashed into a rock. He was driving in the dark, literally peering through blackness and trusting his instincts not to skirt too close to the canyon.

The flashes of lightning had illuminated the trail for the first few miles, but then the storm moved on, leaving only the eerie greenish-black sky. Wind whipped against his face, and Brady constantly had to wipe moisture from his eyes. It might have been more practical for him to take the helmet since he was driving, but he wouldn't have Grace back there freezing. He'd been sent to protect her, but he hadn't done a very good job of it so far.

At least she was still alive, he thought grimly. Which was more than he could say for Rachel.

First Rachel and now Grace. Both witnesses against Stephen Rialto. How had he managed to find Rachel? Was Rialto the one after Grace, or was Kane behind the attack on the cabin?

It didn't much matter. Lester Kane and Stephen Rialto were allies. What helped one helped the other. What tormented Brady now was the breach in security. The fact that two safe houses had been compromised. One witness had already been killed. Someone on the inside was talking.

AS THEY DESCENDED into the foothills, Brady left the trail and took to the open plain. Grace was so numb from the cold, she could hardly hold on to him anymore. She'd never been so miserable in her life, and she could only imagine what it must be like for him, his face unprotected from the freezing wind. She wondered how he kept going, what strength he called on to ignore the wind and the cold and the pain in his arm to get them to safety.

For Grace it was simple. All she had to do was remember her mother's face, the softness of her voice, the way she would sometimes cling to Grace during their visits. No one had ever depended on Grace the way her mother did, and she couldn't let her down. She *couldn't*.

But more and more Grace realized that she might not be able to save her mother alone. She needed Brady's help. He was the only one she could trust, but since the attack on the cabin, she was more frightened than ever. Kane was even more powerful than she'd realized. Brady had said that only a handful of people knew the location of the safe house, which meant someone close to him had to be on Kane's payroll. She couldn't open up to Brady until she was certain he'd cut himself off from his colleagues.

They were slowing, Grace realized suddenly, and with numb hands, she removed the helmet to gaze around at their surroundings. There wasn't much to see. The mountains had receded in the distance, and even in darkness, she could tell that the countryside was flat and barren, with only the occasional silhouette of a mesquite tree to break the infinite terrain.

Brady pulled alongside a barbed wire fence and cut the engine on the ATV. The ensuing silence seemed almost preternatural. An uneasy shiver rippled through Grace.

"Where are we?" Her voice sounded thin and harsh in the quiet.

He lifted his hand and pointed to a spot on the distant horizon. "See that light?"

Grace peered through the darkness in the direction he indicated. She hadn't noticed it before, but there was a tiny yellow pinprick in the blackness.

"That's the Double U ranch house. It's owned by a woman named Maddie Wells."

"Do you know her?"

"She spends a lot of time at the Smoking Barrel."

"Do you trust her?"

Brady hesitated. "I did, until a few hours ago. I don't trust anyone now."

Grace took a measure of comfort in his words. "Why are we here, then?"

"I know this place." Brady's gaze scanned the darkened horizon. "I know the habits of the ranch hands. This is Friday night. Payday. They'll be going into town soon. Maddie's most likely at the Smoking Barrel."

"There's a town around here?" Grace asked in surprise.

"Figure of speech." Brady shrugged. "A saloon.

Mexican restaurant. Post Office. That's about the size of it.''

No bus station or airport, Grace thought. "So what do we do?''

Brady squinted at his watch. "We sit tight for a little while. It's early yet. The men will need time to get cleaned up before they head out.''

They sat for what seemed like hours in the frigid darkness before two tiny lights appeared on the horizon. As the headlights drew closer, Grace could hear the sound of a truck engine. The vehicle passed by them, but she held her breath until the taillights disappeared into the darkness. A few minutes later, another truck roared by, and then another.

Brady started the ATV and headed toward the road. When he stopped at the gate, Grace said, "Won't they hear us coming?''

"Might not be anybody left to hear us, but we'll go on foot from here, just in case.''

He cut the engine again, and both he and Grace climbed off. For a moment, she was afraid her limbs were so deadened she might not be able to walk, but she gritted her teeth and plowed through the darkness behind Brady. He opened the gate, and she stepped gingerly over the cattle guard.

"The house is about two miles down this road,'' he told her, closing the gate behind them. "Think you can make it?''

If he could, with a bullet wound in his arm, then she could. She nodded.

They trudged through the cold until two miles

seemed more like ten, but finally the light in the ranch house grew bigger and brighter. Grace could imagine the cheery warmth inside the sprawling house. There would be food, too. She hadn't eaten since dinner last night. She would give anything for a hot, juicy steak, a steaming baked potato, buttery rolls—

"…wait inside the barn," Brady was saying.

"What?" Barn? What about the ranch house? What about the cheery warmth? The food?

She noticed that he was limping a bit as he guided her toward the barn, and Grace felt guilty for worrying about her own creature comforts. Brady was obviously in a lot of pain, and all she'd been concerned about was her own empty stomach.

The smell of horses and hay, and a few even more earthy scents, assailed Grace's nose as Brady opened the barn door and they stepped inside. She could hear the restless stamp of hooves as the horses sensed their presence.

Any other time, the barn would have probably felt chilly, but after being outside in the wind, the interior was almost comfortable. Brady pointed to a wooden ladder that led up to the hay loft. "Scoot up there while I have a look around. Anyone comes in, you keep out of sight."

He waited until Grace had scrambled up the ladder and given him the thumbs-up sign over the edge of the loft before turning to go back out into the cold.

Grace settled back against the hay, nestling herself into a cozy, little cocoon. She'd almost drifted off to sleep with she heard a faint squeak as the barn door opened, and then a draft of cold air. She thought it was Brady returning and leaned over the edge of the loft to peer down at him. But just as she did so, a beam of light flickered on, and she instinctively shrank back.

Grace could hear the man's soft footfalls as he walked around the barn. Peering between the cracks in the floorboards, she watched the light beam roam about the interior. There was something furtive about the man's movements, something sinister, she thought with a chill.

Somewhere toward the back of the barn, another door opened and an overhead light came on. She burrowed even deeper into the hay as she heard a gruff voice swear violently. "What the hell—

"*Buenes noches,*" the first man said cheerfully. "*Tu eres el encargado?*"

"Speak English, amigo. You're across the border now."

The first man laughed without offense. "Nice spread you have here. Are you the boss man?"

"I'm the foreman, but what's it to you?"

"I'm looking for a friend of mine. He came out this way looking for work."

"Work?" the foreman scoffed. "This time of year?" Grace couldn't see his face, but she could imagine his features—grizzled hair, deeply lined face from years of working in blistering heat and bone-chilling cold. "We can barely keep our regulars busy."

"Maybe you saw my friend just the same," the first man said in his accented English. "Tall man. Dark hair. About my age." He paused. "His name is Morgan. Brady Morgan. He's traveling with a woman."

"Morgan? Why, hell. You got the wrong damn ranch. Morgan's over at the Smoking Barrel. But he ain't no new hire. He's been there for years—"

There was a soft *spit-spit,* and then Grace heard the sound of a body hitting the floor. Below, the horses began to prance and snort, distressed by the intrusion. Inside her chest, Grace's heart flailed like a caged bird.

The man below was a killer, and he'd referred to Brady by name. He'd come looking for them, which meant, in all probability, that Kane knew Grace was with Brady. If Kane assumed she'd talked, there'd be nothing stopping him from killing her mother. Maybe he already had—

Almost too late, Grace realized the killer was at the bottom of the ladder. She heard his foot move to the first rung, and then the next. In a moment, he would be in the loft, and there was nowhere for Grace to hide. Nowhere to run.

She glanced around frantically. Images of those mass graves in Juarez flashed through her mind. The young college students who had been mutilated by the drug cartel in Matamoras. The people in the drug trade were violent, ruthless savages. She would be killed for what she knew, but not instantly. First, she would be convinced to turn over the tape—

The killer was near the top now. Grace could hear him breathing. Or was that her own breath, coming in short, gasping jerks? She tried to sink farther into the hay, and as she did, her hand met something wooden. A handle—

Instantly, she was on her feet. The killer rose through the opening, balancing himself on the ladder as his gaze lit on her. He had dark hair, black eyes, and the whitest teeth Grace had ever seen as he grinned at her.

"Por fin, nos conocemos."

"The pleasure is all mine." Grace lunged toward him, swinging the pitchfork with all her might. Blood spurted from his forehead, covering her, and for an instant he stood balanced on the ladder, looking nothing more than dazed. Then, without a sound, he toppled backward.

He landed at the bottom of the ladder with a sickening thud. Breathless with terror, Grace scrabbled over to the edge and peered down. Brady, the dead man at his feet, gazed up at her.

BRADY CHECKED the foreman's pulse. The man was new to the Double U, not someone Brady had known well. Only an acquaintance who had been in the wrong place at the wrong time. Another victim of the drug wars when Brady doubted the man had ever taken anything stronger than an aspirin. A belt of whiskey, maybe, for snakebite, chills, whatever other ailment might have come along.

He closed the man's eyes, wishing he could call Maddie and let her know what had happened, but he didn't have time for that. Besides, it was like he'd told Grace earlier. He couldn't afford to trust anyone. Not Maddie, not Mitchell. No one.

Grace was still in the loft, and when Brady climbed the ladder he saw that she was sitting with her head between her knees, fighting nausea. He called her name softly, but she didn't look up. He was afraid she might be going into shock, and they didn't have time for that, either.

He walked over and knelt beside her, taking her shoulders in his hands. "Grace?"

She glanced up at him then, her eyes red-rimmed and dazed.

"You okay?"

"I don't know." She clutched her stomach, bending low. "Oh, God, I think I'm going to be sick."

He held her head while she vomited into the hay. Maddie's ranch hands were going to be in for more than one bad surprise when they showed up for work in the morning, Brady thought grimly.

When Grace was finished, he wiped her face gently with his handkerchief, then pulled her to her feet. "Come on, honey. We have to get out of here."

She trembled from head to toe. "I killed him. Brady, I killed someone."

"He would have killed you. You know that."

She put her hands to her face. Brady wondered if she realized they were bloodstained. He took her hands in his and drew them away. "You did what you had to do."

"I killed him with a pitchfork. Oh, God." She closed her eyes, swaying. "All that blood—"

"Grace." His voice was harsher now. He had to get through to her. They had to get out of there. "Listen to me. He would have killed you. He probably would have killed me. You did what you had to do."

"I know, but—"

"It'll be all right. I promise." He smoothed his hand down her hair, wishing he could take her in his arms, make her pain go away. But he knew from experience that the nightmares wouldn't go away for a very long time. "There's a truck outside. We need to get going."

She nodded numbly. Brady went first down the ladder, and when they were at the bottom, he tried to turn her quickly so that she wouldn't see the dead man on the floor. But he was hard to avoid, and so was the blood. Grace began to shake violently.

Brady wrapped his arm around her and guided her quickly toward the back of the barn. "The truck's out back. I left the motor running, so it should be warm inside."

When they passed the foreman's body, Grace whispered, "He didn't do anything. He was killed for no reason."

"Just like hundreds of others have been. Drug

trafficking is an ugly business, Grace. These men are brutal.''

She nodded, but he couldn't tell if his words were getting through to her or not. Outside, the wind had risen, and Brady could hear the clatter of a nearby windmill. He opened the truck door for Grace, and she climbed inside.

Once he'd gotten in on the other side, she seemed to rally. She glanced around the cab. ''Whose truck is this?''

Brady hesitated, thinking she might not really want the truth. ''One of the ranch hands.''

''How did you get the key?''

''I didn't. I hot-wired it.''

She glanced at him, a faint smile tugging at her pale lips. ''Hot-wired it? Where did you learn to do that?''

''In my juvenile days on the street. Some of those bad habits come in handy now and then.'' New vehicles were almost impossible to hot-wire, but older models, like this one, were a piece of cake.

Brady put the truck into gear and they pulled away from the barn. Neither one of them spoke again until they got to the gate, and he stopped the truck to open it. Grace climbed out with him.

''I'll close it after you pull through.''

He started to protest, but then shrugged. ''Thanks.''

The tires drummed over the metal cattle guard, and he watched in his rearview mirror as Grace wrestled with the gate in the wind. Finally she had it fastened, and she climbed back in, slamming her door.

"All set."

"We're off then." Brady glanced at her worriedly. She still looked way too pale to suit him. He pulled a bottle from beneath the seat and handed it to her.

"What is it?" she asked reluctantly.

"Whiskey. I don't have a cup, but the seal hasn't been broken. The bottle's clean."

She tried to twist open the lid, but her hands were trembling too badly. She handed the bottle back to him. "Sorry. I can't seem to stop shaking."

"This'll help." He opened the whiskey and passed it back to her.

She stared at the bottle for a moment, then turned it up.

"Careful," Brady warned. "You're drinking on an empty stomach." He could have used a belt himself, but until they got to where they were going, he had to keep a clear head.

He glanced at her again. "There's a place south of here no one else knows about. We'll head for that."

"You're not going to report back to your people?"

"No. From here on out, we're on our own, Grace." Out of the corner of his eye, he saw her take another quick swig of whiskey.

"Brady?"

"Yeah?"

"You were right. I have been holding out on you."

"I'm listening." He was relieved to hear that her voice sounded almost back to normal.

"Kane is threatening me."

"He's using your mother, right?"

She nodded. "Yes, but it's worse that you thought. He has her. He took her from the nursing home, and I don't know where she is. If she's all right—" Her voice broke, and Brady saw her draw the back of her hand across her face.

He scowled at the road, trying to ignore the throbbing in his arm and focus on the problem at hand. It *was* worse than he thought. The likelihood that Grace's mother was still alive wasn't all that great. She had to know that. "When did this happen?"

"The same morning I witnessed the murder. After I'd called the police from Burt's office, I went back home to my apartment. Kane called me on my cell phone. I don't even know how he got my number."

Cell phone numbers weren't that hard to acquire, if you knew how to go about it. Neither were unlisted numbers. Especially if Kane had someone on the inside working for him. "Did he let you talk to her?"

"No. All he said was that he had people in places I couldn't begin to imagine. If I talked to anyone, including the police, he'd know it. And he'd kill my mother. That's why I didn't tell you. I trusted you, but I didn't know who you were working for, and I was worried that someone in your organization might report back to Kane. And Brady—'' She turned to face him. ''I was right to be worried. That man back there…he knew you. He called you by name. He told the foreman he was looking for you.''

Damn, Brady thought. He could no longer deny the leak was coming from his end. All they could do now was find a place to try and regroup.

''Yesterday at the cabin…you thought I'd made a phone call. I didn't,'' Grace said. ''But I did get my voice mail. I had a message from Kane. Saturday, Dealey Plaza, 6:00 p.m. That's all he said. Tomorrow is Saturday, Brady. I have to get back there. I can't miss that meeting. My mother's life depends on it.''

''Are you sure the message was from Kane?''

''The voice was garbled, but who else could it be? He said he'd be in touch. He said he'd set up an exchange. The tape for my mother. Who else would have left me that message?''

It was a trap, of course. Grace wasn't just smart, she was street-savvy. She had to know the chances of Kane letting her mother go—of him letting Grace go—were nil. If she went to that meeting, she'd be walking into an ambush.

There was no way Brady could allow that. He had to keep her as far away from Dealey Plaza as possible on Saturday, but she was right about one thing. They did have to go back to Dallas. That tape was the way to lure Kane out into the open.

''All right,'' he said finally. ''We'll go back to

Dallas. We'll get the tape. We'll deal with Kane only...we do it my way. Agreed?''

She started to protest, but then thought better of it. Brady didn't buy her submission for a moment. He could almost read her mind. Once she got back to Dallas, the rules would change. He knew her better than she thought he did, which kept him for the time being at least, one step ahead of her.

THE SECLUDED cabin Brady pulled up to looked hardly more than a tumbledown shack. Grace got out of the truck and stared at it doubtfully. "Who owns this place?"

"I do."

"You?" She glanced at him in surprise. *"Why?"*

She sensed more than saw his grin in the darkness. "Because it's remote. Because no one knows about it but me. I like to come out here to be by myself. Do some thinking."

Grace hesitated to point out to him that he could go almost any place in West Texas and be by himself. But this place was even more remote than the other cabin. They looked to be in the middle of the desert, with nothing but the silhouette of low-lying hills to break the endless horizon. The countryside seemed almost alien to her. "We must be close to the border," she said, gazing around.

"Just a few miles south of here." He nodded toward the hills. "There used to be a big ranch house just over that first hill. That's why we've got electricity out here. When the house burned, the owner sold out. I got the property for a song, but I haven't had time to rebuild." He shrugged, unconcerned. "The cabin suits my purposes anyway."

He unlocked the door, and they stepped inside. The light was a bare bulb suspended from the ceiling. Brady turned it on by pulling a string connected to the socket.

The harsh lighting did little to alleviate the primitive interior. There was no furniture to speak of, just a wooden table and two chairs, a gas cookstove, an ancient refrigerator, a porcelain sink, and a stone fireplace.

The place was freezing on the inside. Grace shivered as she gazed around.

"I'll get a fire started," Brady said. "Meanwhile, I do have hot water out here, believe it or not. There's a bathroom of sorts, if you want to get cleaned up."

She gazed down at her hands and saw the dried blood. Her stomach quivered sickeningly.

The tiny bathroom Brady showed her was almost as rustic as the rest of cabin, but it did have running water, a toilet, and a sink. The shower was handheld, with a drain in the middle of the floor. By the time Grace was finished, she'd managed to get everything wet, including her clothes, which she'd kicked into a pile in the corner.

Wrapping a towel around her, she opened the door to find that Brady had left a stack of clothing on the floor. She dressed quickly, shivering as she drew on the flannel shirt—his, obviously—a pair of boxer shorts—also his, she hoped—and a pair of thick socks.

Brady was at the stove, stirring something in a pan. He glanced up when she joined him, his gaze taking in her borrowed getup. "Didn't figure any of my jeans would fit you," he said, turning back to the stove.

"You keep clothes out here?" She glanced around, still unable to imagine Brady spending time in this place.

"Yeah, but they keep disappearing. Sometimes people coming over the border stumble onto this place and break in. They take the clothes, and whatever else I've left lying around. Razors, toothbrushes, you name it."

"I found a spare toothbrush in the bathroom," Grace said. "I hope you don't mind that I used it."

He shrugged and flashed her a grin. "I've got another stashed around here somewhere. I've gotten pretty good at finding hiding places. Lucky I put away a can of soup or two."

He removed the pan from the stove and carried it over to the table. "Hope you like chicken noodle."

Grace didn't think she could put anything in her stomach, but she also knew that if she didn't eat, she'd only get weaker. And that wouldn't do. She'd need all her strength tomorrow.

Brady fished out another spoon from a drawer. "All the bowls have walked off," he said. "Dining will be very informal this evening."

They ate the soup right out of the pan, and the

nourishing broth and noodles managed to restore Grace's appetite. After the first tentative bite or two, she ate with relish.

Afterward, she washed the pan and spoons in the sink while Brady had his turn in the shower. "You probably shouldn't get your arm wet," she'd admonished, when he'd headed for the bathroom.

He glanced over his shoulder, his expression ironic. "That's the least of my worries right now."

Still, Grace was concerned. His injury wouldn't be life-threatening if treated properly, but all she'd been able to do was clean away the blood and use a piece of her shirt for a bandage. Nothing had been sterilized. It would be a miracle if infection didn't set in.

She didn't know how he managed to keep going. How he'd climbed down on that ledge in the canyon to get her. How he'd driven the four-wheeler back to the cabin to get their coats. How he'd faced down a mountain lion, hot-wired a truck, and helped her keep her sanity after she'd—

Grace didn't want to remember what had happened in that hayloft, but she knew she would never forget. Her sleep would be haunted for a long time to come, and if it hadn't been for Brady, she might have really lost it back there.

But he'd kept her going. He'd kept himself going. And now, hurt arm and all, he was going to help her save her mother.

Only one problem there, though. If Kane knew

that Brady was at that drop tomorrow, he'd never show. Angeline wouldn't stand a chance.

Grace drew a long breath. She needed Brady to help her get back to Dallas. But once they were there, she'd have to find a way to meet Kane on her own.

Chapter Thirteen

While Grace had been in the shower, Brady had laid out sleeping bags in front of the fireplace. She climbed into one now, settling herself into the folds as she stared at the ceiling. The cabin was finally warm, and she felt almost cozy. The flickering fire, combined with the whiskey, made her grow drowsy, and she'd just drifted off when Brady came out of the bathroom.

He climbed into the sleeping bag beside her and settled down with a weary sigh. Grace raised herself on one elbow. "Brady?"

"Yeah?"

"I found a first-aid kit in the kitchen. I think we should put some disinfectant on your arm. I'm worried about infection."

"It'll be fine. Let's just get some sleep."

"Come on. It'll only take a minute."

He gave another weary sigh as he tossed back the sleeping bag and sat up. He was shirtless, and the jeans he wore rode low on his hips. Firelight flickered over the muscle definition in his arms and shoulders, and for a moment, Grace was mesmerized by the tautness of his stomach, the sprinkling of hair that arrowed beneath the waist of his jeans. "Make it quick," he said irritably, snapping Grace's attention back. "We need to get some rest. We've got a long day ahead of us tomorrow."

What was probably going to be their last day together, she thought with a pang. She tried not to dwell on the inevitable, but instead, on the task at hand. She got up and turned on the light. Brady got up and brought the bottle of whiskey from the table. He took a long swig as she set to work.

She tried to make it quick, but his arm was a mess. The wound didn't appear deep, but it was nasty-looking, with jagged edges where the flesh had literally been ripped apart.

Shuddering, she dabbed at the wound with a saturated cotton ball, and the moment the disinfectant came into contact with raw flesh, Brady sucked in a sharp breath. "*Damn,* Grace. Maybe you should just shoot me instead."

"Sorry." She glanced up apologetically. "I know this hurts."

"Just get on with it," he said through gritted teeth. He took another pull on the whiskey bottle. Grace noticed the contents were well below half. How much of the damage had she done herself?

She set to work again, and this time, when she tried to touch the cotton ball to his arm, Brady jerked it away.

"I didn't even touch it yet!" she said impatiently.

"Yes, you did. You touched it plenty. I'm good to go. Let's just get some rest."

"Oh, for heaven's sake," she said in exasperation. "How can you have survived everything you've been through in the last couple of days and be such a baby about this?"

"Because you're making it worse," Brady said darkly. "My arm felt fine until you started messing with it."

"Just hold still." Grace, cotton ball poised in her hand, rolled her eyes skyward. Wasn't that just like a man? Stoic through flying bullets, mountain lions, and assassins, but try putting a little medicine on an injury and they acted like two-year-olds. It amused her a little to realize that Brady Morgan—cop, cowboy, undercover agent—was no exception.

"Just give me another minute," she murmured, dabbing the wound quickly. She taped on a gauze bandage. "There. That's the best I can do under the circumstances."

"Thanks," he said dryly.

When she got up to turn off the light, he grabbed her hand. "Not so fast."

"What is it?"

"That cut on your head could use a little attention, too."

"What?" She lifted her hand to her forehead. After everything else that had happened, Grace had forgotten about the scrape she'd gotten earlier that morning. Other than the occasional twinge, it hadn't bothered her. "It's just a scratch."

"It's more than that, and besides, we have to worry about infection. Let's put a little disinfectant on it, just to be on the safe side."

She stared at him suspiciously. "What is this, revenge?"

"Just being cautious." Brady got a fresh cotton ball and dabbed it with disinfectant. Before he even touched Grace's forehead, she drew back. "What's the matter?" he said. "Not afraid of a little disinfectant, are you?"

She gritted her teeth, just as he had. "Okay. Do it." He touched her gently, but the medicine set the cut on fire. She grabbed the whiskey bottle and took a long drink.

"Hurts like hell, doesn't it?"

"Yes, smart aleck."

He grinned. "But now we're both germ-free, we can get some sleep."

He got up and turned off the light. When he'd gotten settled again in the sleeping bag, Grace said, "Brady?"

"Yeah?"

"Thanks."

"For the disinfectant?"

"For everything. You saved my life earlier."

He hesitated for a moment. "I don't know, Grace. You handled yourself pretty well. I'm beginning to think you may have been better off if I'd left you in Dallas."

She turned to gaze at him in the firelight. "Meaning?"

"The trouble started when I came on the scene."

She sighed, turning her head to stare at the ceiling. "No. The trouble started when I went to the warehouse that night. I'm not naive. I know Kane intends to kill my mother and me. Once he has the tape, he'll come after us. That's why we have to disappear."

"You could do that in the Witness Protection Program."

"With someone on the inside on Kane's payroll? I don't think so. You know as well as I do he'd find a way to get to me. I'd never live long enough to testify."

He was silent for a long time, and then Grace felt his hand close over hers. "I'm going to help you out of this mess, Grace. You and your mother both. Trust me."

"I do."

She did trust Brady, with her very life. But unfortunately, he wasn't the one calling the shots. Kane was.

A NIGHTMARE awakened Grace. She and her mother were running through Dealey Plaza. Kane was pursuing them with a pitchfork. Her mother fell, and Grace helped her to her feet, but her mother couldn't walk, and Grace couldn't carry her. Kane was closing in on them, and there was nothing she could do. She could hear Brady calling to her, but he was too far away to reach them in time. He couldn't help her. Grace was on her own—

She sat up, trying to clear the remnants of the dream from her head. It was getting cold inside the cabin. The fire had died down, and she started to get up to put on another log. A low moan from Brady halted her. She thought at first he was in pain, but then she realized he was in the throes of his own nightmare.

''Don't die!''

He was dreaming about his father again. Grace knelt beside him. She lifted her hand to touch his chest, to gently awaken him, but she froze when he said a name.

''Rachel! Oh, God, Rachel!''

The desperation and fear in his voice almost stopped Grace's heart. Who was Rachel?

Someone Brady had been involved with after he'd left Grace? Someone he'd been in love with?

It was agonizing to think of him in another woman's arms, although Grace knew she had no right to think of him as hers. Not after what she'd done. If Brady had found someone else after her, then it only served her right.

But it still hurt. The thought of it still killed her, because in five years, there had been no one else for her.

He groaned again, and Grace gently shook him awake. ''Brady?''

He bolted upright, grabbing her, his gaze frantically searching her face.

He thinks I'm Rachel, she thought.

His gaze seemed to clear then, and his grip slackened. "What's wrong?"

"Nothing. You were having a nightmare. Calling out in your sleep."

He looked disturbed by her words. "Sorry if I woke you up," he muttered, getting up to throw another log onto the fire. He busied himself at the fireplace for a few moments before coming back to lie down beside her.

Grace propped herself on her elbow, staring at his profile. His skin had been hot to touch. She wondered if he had a fever, or if the pain in his arm had provoked the nightmare.

"Brady?"

When he didn't say anything, Grace lay back and gazed at the ceiling. "Who's Rachel?"

He still didn't say anything. She turned her head to stare at him. His eyes were closed, but she knew he hadn't gone back to sleep. In the light from the fire, she could see the telltale tightening of his features, the tiny frown that played between his brows. Obviously, Rachel was a subject he didn't care to discuss.

When she'd given up on him answering her, he said almost brusquely, "She was a witness I was assigned to protect."

"What happened?"

"She died."

"How?"

He glanced at her then, his gaze almost angry. "It's not something I like to talk about, okay?"

Grace nodded. "I understand. But you still dream about her. Whatever happened obviously still bothers you a great deal. Maybe it would help to talk about it."

"You're not a shrink, Grace."

She flinched at his harsh words. "No. But I am someone who cares about you."

His gaze softened slightly before he turned away. He lay on his back, staring at the ceiling. After a moment, he said, "She was Stephen Rialto's mistress. Last year she decided to turn state's evidence, and I was assigned to protect her until she could testify."

"Like me."

"But unlike you, Rachel was cooperating," he said. "Security was breached. The safe house where we were staying came under attack one night."

"Déjà vu," Grace whispered.

His voice grew even more grim. "Except Rachel was killed. That's not going to happen to you."

"Were you wounded?"

He shrugged, but didn't answer.

"Is that what happened to your leg?" Grace persisted. "I've noticed you limping from time to time."

"It tore up my knee pretty badly," he said. "I had several months of physical therapy. There was a time when I wasn't certain I'd ever walk again."

"But you did." She had an image of Brady in a

rehab center, fighting for each step. Fighting to regain his life, his independence, his dignity. Brady, who had always seemed so invincible to her. Grace blinked back tears as she glanced at him tenderly. "You've been through a lot."

"I'm alive. That's more than I can say for Rachel."

There was pain and guilt in his voice, but also something else. Grief?

"Were you in love with her?" She asked the question so softly, she wasn't certain he'd heard her, but he turned his head and met her gaze. His eyes were shadowed by an emotion Grace thought was regret.

"Witness protection is a tricky thing," he said. "You're confined to close quarters night and day. You get to know a person in ways you wouldn't under ordinary circumstances. You come to rely on one another, and sometimes a bond forms. An intimacy—"

Grace turned away. "I don't need to hear the details."

She felt his hand on her arm. His touch was soft, gentle. Reassuring. "It wasn't what you're thinking. We didn't sleep together. But there was…something."

Grace closed her eyes. "I guess I always knew you'd find someone else. I just never thought…I never knew it would hurt this much."

"The bond that Rachel and I had…" He paused, as if unsure what to say to her. How to explain his feelings. "It was nothing compared to what you and I had, Grace."

Had was the key word, as he'd once told her. She opened her eyes and gazed up at him. He was sitting up, propped on one elbow as he watched the fire. Grace thought that she had never loved him more than she did at that moment, even knowing about Rachel. Even knowing that come tomorrow, they might never see each other again. Or maybe it was because of all those things. Maybe everything they'd both been through in the last five years had made her appreciate the man Brady was more than she ever had before.

"Was Rachel going into the Witness Protection Program after she testified?"

Brady seemed surprised by the question. "It was already set up. Why?"

"You would have let her go like that? You would never have seen her again?"

"That's the way it works, Grace. I wouldn't have had a choice."

"With me, either."

He realized what she was getting at then, and he turned back to the fire, his expression stark. "If you testify against Kane, then you'll be given a new identify. A new life. I won't know your new name or where you've been sent."

"And if I don't testify, if I make the exchange with Kane and take my mother out of the country, we'll still never see each other again, will we?"

His gaze met hers. "Probably not."

She turned to stare at the fire for a moment. "There's something I want to say to you then."

"Grace—"

"No, don't stop me. I need to say this." She rose to kneel beside him. "I've never stopped caring about you, Brady. For the last five years, all I ever wanted was your forgiveness." When he tried to protest, she said quickly, "I'm not saying this to try and con you. I don't have any ulterior motives. I love you and think I always will."

She touched his cheek with her fingertips. "I just wanted you to know. After tomorrow, we may never see each other again."

He caught her hand and drew her fingers to his lips. The way he looked at her made her pulse race. He said very softly, "We still have tonight."

THE YEARS melted away as rapidly as their clothing. They lay naked on top of the sleeping bags, kissing and touching as the passion built to a fevered pitch. It was different now, though. Where once Brady would have succumbed to the urgency of the moment, he held back, savoring the feel and the taste and the beauty of Grace's lean body.

Her legs were long and slender, like a dancer's, and her strength only complemented her femininity. She was strong and capable, a warrior woman at times, but she could be submissive when he wanted her to be. Demanding, when he needed her to be. She stroked him knowingly, and Brady lay back, his body on fire, as Grace rose over him, an Amazon queen ready to conquer.

But it wasn't going to be quite that easy, he decided. He reached up, cupping the back of her neck to pull her toward him, kissing her until she collapsed against him, her strength waning with desire.

"Brady..." she whispered weakly.

They were lying side by side now, and Brady knew that she was being careful not to hurt his arm. But the whiskey had dulled the pain, and with Grace naked against him, there were more pressing aches. More urgent needs.

He rose over her now, kissing her again, whispering in her ear, making her tell him what she wanted. And she complied. Wrapping her long legs around him, she left no doubt.

As their bodies melded, Brady thought his heart might pound its way right out of his chest.

GRACE LAY back against the sleeping bag and sighed. Her heart was still racing. She put her hand to her chest, measuring the beat, as she watched shadows dance across the ceiling.

Beside her, Brady stirred, settling himself on the sleeping bag. She could feel his gaze on her, and she smiled lazily. "That was incredible."

"It always was."

"Yes, but this time..." She turned to face him. "It was different this time."

"I know."

"Brady—" She took his hand, drawing it to her

face. "I'll never forget this night. I'll dream about it."

He gazed down at their linked hands, a shadow passing over his features. "Tomorrow…today," he amended, glancing at his watch. "After the exchange, if you still want to leave the country with your mother, I'll help you."

"What about the Witness Protection Program?" she asked in surprise.

"You were right. Unless we find the leak, it's too dangerous. Kane found you once. I won't take a chance on him finding you again."

"You think one of your colleagues is on the take?"

He rubbed a hand across his tired eyes. "I don't know. The men I work with…I'd trust any one of them with my life. They're good men, Grace. Dedicated. I have a hard time believing any of them would have turned."

"You know them all that well?"

"They're like my family." He got up and stirred the fire, then came back to lay down beside her, pulling one of the sleeping bags over them. Grace snuggled against him, drawing warmth from his body and strength from his presence.

"What you said before…about tomorrow." She turned to glance at him. "You said, 'from here on out, it's just you and me'. I'm glad you're with me, Brady. You have no idea how much."

Grace felt his lips skim her hair. "I'm glad, too."

"Things have changed between us, haven't they?" she murmured. "Or is it just me?"

"No. Things are different. We're different."

"But it's too late."

"That's the hell of it, isn't it?" His voice was heavy with regret.

Grace turned in his arms. His gaze was so tender she felt everything still inside her. "We still have tonight," she whispered, fighting back tears.

Chapter Fourteen

They woke up early, quickly showered and dressed, and were on the road by dawn. They took Highway 17 all the way to Pecos, and from there Interstate 80 to Odessa. The trip took nearly four hours, including a stop for gas, food, and a change of clothing for Grace. The flight to Dallas took less than half that time. At Love Field, they rented a car, and by one o'clock had checked into a downtown hotel, in a room overlooking Dealey Plaza.

By three o'clock, Brady was already watching the area through binoculars he'd picked up at a camera store a few blocks away, and the tape had been retrieved from a locker at the bus station. The only thing missing was Grace and her mother's passports, which were in a safety-deposit box at the bank. No way to get to them until Monday, when the bank opened, but they wouldn't wait that long. She and her mother would head for New York immediately, hide out until she could contact her father, and then, with his contacts, he would help them get the necessary papers.

She paced the room nervously, realizing the plan was not without fault. Her father might refuse to cooperate. And even if he did, he might not be as powerful and well-connected as she'd always thought. A million things could go wrong, but the most dangerous element was the exchange itself. As soon as he had his hands on the tape, Kane would want them dead. Somehow Grace had to make sure she and her mother were out of the line of fire before Kane got the tape.

Brady glanced at her over his shoulder. "You're as nervous as a cat. Why don't you go take a hot bath, try to relax. I've got this covered."

Grace started to protest, but he was right. She had to calm herself down before the meeting.

Going into the bathroom, she stripped as the tub filled. Settling herself into the steamy water, she closed her eyes, willing away the tension as she ran over the coming scenario in her mind. She and Brady already had a car waiting in a lot near Dealey Plaza for the escape. Brady would provide cover. On that point he had been insistent. He would never let her go to that meeting alone, but Grace was worried about that. He'd already been watching the area for signs of Kane and his men for the better part of an hour. Kane would probably be doing the same. If he caught a glimpse of Brady, or any cop, then Angeline would be killed.

Somehow, Grace would have to find a way to get

rid of Brady. She'd have to go to that meeting alone, but that meant she might never see him again. Once she and her mother left for New York, there would be no turning back. Brady would be gone from her life forever.

Feeling depressed and scared, Grace climbed out of the tub, quickly dried off, and pulled on her clothes. Suddenly, she couldn't wait to see Brady again, but when she opened the bathroom door and stepped out, the hotel room was empty.

She glanced around, dismayed. Then her gaze lit on the bed. The tape was missing. Brady had taken it, but...why? He couldn't go to that meeting in Grace's place. Kane would never show. So why had he taken the tape?

To turn over to the DPS? Did putting Kane away mean so much to him that he was willing risk Angeline's life?

Grace didn't want to believe it, but the fact remained that the tape was gone. She'd never felt so betrayed.

ALL THE WHILE he and Grace had made the arrangements for the meeting with Kane, Brady had known in the back of his mind that there was no way he'd let her go to Dealey Plaza. Kane would never allow her and her mother to walk away alive, and if he had the place surrounded, which was likely, a dozen getaway cars wouldn't make a difference. The meeting was an ambush, pure and simple, but Grace was so desperate to rescue her mother, she was willing to put her own life on the line. Brady couldn't let her do it.

But as he'd watched the street from their hotel window, he'd gone over and over in his mind everything he'd ever known about Lester Kane. Five years ago, he'd gone undercover to expose Kane's operation, and he'd managed to get on the inside. He'd learned of drop-off points, warehouses Kane had used for distribution, even most of the small-time street dealers who had worked for Kane. But none of it had mattered once Grace's story had run prematurely because everything had disappeared. Evidence. Witnesses. Everything. They hadn't been able to touch Kane, and Brady had thought the information he'd learned was useless, the hours he'd spent on the case wasted.

But as he'd gazed at the street below their hotel window, something had come back to him. Kane had a sister named Delia. Five years ago she'd worked as a registered nurse at Parkland Memorial Hospital. Brady had even staked out her house one night, watching for Kane.

He thought about that now as he parked the car down the block, and stared at the same house. He had no idea whether or not Delia Kane still lived at the same address, but who better to take care of a hostage with Alzheimer's than a registered nurse?

He got out of the car and crossed the street, walking the half block or so to the house. The sky was overcast. Even though it was only four-thirty or so, darkness was already falling. But no light shone from any of the windows. He wondered if Delia was still at work.

Glancing over his shoulder, he rounded the house and let himself in through the back gate. A dog barked next door, and he quickly moved into the shadows on the concrete patio.

The door was secured, but the lock was flimsy. Brady was inside in less than a minute. Drawing his weapon, he moved silently from room to room, thinking fleetingly that with all the money Kane made from drugs, his sister's home was pretty modest, a tract house with the same floor plan he'd seen hundreds of times.

Maybe Delia Kane wouldn't take drug money. Maybe she wouldn't be involved in a kidnapping, either.

In the living room, he moved to the window and checked the street. Then he turned and headed down a narrow hallway toward the bedrooms. All the doors were open except for the one at the end of the hallway. As Brady's hand closed around the knob, he heard something stir within, a rustling sound that spiked his adrenaline.

He shoved open the door and planted himself, weapon raised. The woman sitting in the gloom stared at him in confusion. Her blue eyes looked familiar, but her hair had gone completely white. Grace's mother was only in her mid-fifties, but she'd aged since Brady had last seen her. So much so, he almost didn't recognize her.

Her puzzled eyes met his, and she lifted her fingertips to her chin, as if trying to figure out what was going on. Slowly, Brady lowered his gun and put it away. He crossed the floor and knelt beside her chair.

"Mrs. Drummond?"

She cocked her head slightly, trying to place him.

"I'm Brady Morgan. We met once. Your daughter, Grace introduced us."

"Grace," the woman said softly and smiled.

Brady nodded. "I'm going to take you to Grace. Would you like that?"

Her fingers reached out to touch his face. Then her gaze lifted, and Brady realized, too late, that someone had come into the room behind him. Someone wearing soft-soled shoes. Nurse's shoes.

He had a glimpse of white as he spun, but the woman was quick. She crashed a crystal vase with all her might against Brady's skull.

GRACE STOOD near the reflecting pool on Elm Street, her gaze sweeping the area for signs of Kane. From her vantage, she could see the Grassy Knoll and the three-layered overpass beyond. She also had a view of the John F. Kennedy Memorial in the middle of Commerce Street and the lighted window of the Fifth Floor Museum, located in the building which had once been known as the Texas Book Depository.

The Mavericks were in town, and the streets were littered with fans walking from dinner on the West End to Reunion Arena. The interstate was crowded as well, and Grace wondered if that would help or hinder her and her mother's escape.

Who was she kidding? she thought in despair. Without that tape, the possibility of getting out of this alive was almost nil. But she wouldn't be able to live with herself if she didn't try. Her mother would have done no less for her.

It was almost six o'clock, and Grace had seen no sign of Kane. Walking down Commerce, she crossed to the middle of the street. The memorial was a boxy structure with thirty-foot-high concrete walls, elevated slightly off the ground, and two narrow openings, north and south, through which to enter and exit. Inside, the cenotaph was sterile, devoid of ornamentation. A space designed for quiet reflection.

Grace glanced over her shoulder, then stepped inside. Someone was already in there, gazing at the inscription on a slab of gray granite.

When the figure turned, Grace gasped, "What are you doing here?"

BRADY GROANED as he tentatively felt the back of his head. A goose egg had popped out at the base of his skull, but he wasn't bleeding. At least, not much. Fighting off a wave of dizziness, he struggled to his feet.

It was dark in the room, but light filtered in through the window, sparking off the bits of broken glass on the floor. Angeline was in bed, her eyes closed, sleeping peacefully.

Brady felt her pulse. It was slow and slightly erratic. He wondered if she'd been drugged.

Crossing to the door, he opened it a crack and peered out. He could see up the hallway to the lighted living room where a television played softly in the background. Delia Kane, still in her nurse's uniform, paced the room, a cordless phone to her ear and his gun dangling from her other hand. Her voice rose in distress.

"What do you mean, you don't know where he is? Find him, for God's sake!"

A pause, then, "Look, I don't care what you have to do, but you find my brother and tell him to get over here now. They're both out, but I don't know for how long. I'm not going to be responsible for this. I'm not going to be a party to murder—"

She halted, as if she'd been interrupted. She listened for a moment, then slammed the phone down angrily. Turning, she strode down the hallway. Brady closed the door and lay back down on the floor. When she entered the room, she nudged him with her foot, then moved to the bed to check on Angeline. She placed the gun on the nightstand as she leaned over the sleeping woman. Brady rose silently and grabbed her by the throat, applying enough pressure to make her see spots as he brought the gun up to her temple. The woman struggled for a moment, then went slack.

"Where's Kane?"

He loosened his hold to allow her to answer, but

she shook her head. "I'm not telling you anything," she gasped.

"Then you aren't much use to me."

Dragging her over to the closet, Brady pushed her inside, then shoved a chair beneath the knob. Instead of pounding on the door and screaming, the woman went absolutely silent. Her brother had taught her well, Brady thought grimly. The woman knew how to keep her mouth shut.

Quickly, he picked up Angeline, but from the window in the living room, he saw a car cruise down the street. Before it had time to pull up outside, Brady had already reversed directions and headed for the back door. Angeline wasn't as tall as her daughter, and she weighed hardly anything. Under ordinary circumstances, Brady could have carried her easily. But these were hardly ordinary circumstances. His knee had withstood too much stress in the last few days, and his arm was screaming in agony. On top of that, he had one helluva headache.

"I think I'm getting too old for this," he murmured to Grace's mother as he carried her out of the house into the darkness.

"SO...THE MESSAGE was from you?" Grace asked, still in shock at seeing her friend instead of Kane.

Helen nodded. "I'm sorry, Grace. I didn't know how else to get in touch with you. I was so worried. I thought if we could meet, I might be able to help you."

Grace felt as if her whole world were crashing in

on her. Her legs almost buckled, and Helen grabbed her arm, supporting her as she pulled her into a corner, away from a group of tourists that had entered the memorial.

"Grace, what is it?" Helen asked desperately. "What's happened to you? You look terrible!"

"I thought the message was from Kane," she said weakly. "It didn't sound like your voice and Kane wants the tape—"

"You brought the tape?" Helen cut in urgently. "You have it?"

Something in Helen's demeanor, in the excited gleam of her dark eyes, alarmed Grace. She stared down at her friend. "No. It's hidden. I'm not stupid enough to have it on me."

Helen's eyes flickered for a moment as her grasp tightened on Grace's arm. A man detached himself from the group of tourists and came toward them. He wore a long overcoat, and one of his hands was stuffed in his pocket. As he approached them, Grace could see his face, and recognition flickered through her. She couldn't place him, but she knew she'd seen him before.

"Does she have it?" His tone was low and menacing. Grace knew his voice, too. He was the man who had been in the warehouse with Kane the night he murdered Alec Priestley. The man she thought was Stephen Rialto.

In a heartbeat, everything Grace had ever heard about Rialto flashed through her mind. Brutal, brilliant, cold-blooded. The hopelessness of her situation stole over her, threatening her courage.

She gazed at Helen in horror. "Why?"

She ignored Grace's question. "She doesn't have the tape on her. She hid it. She didn't say where."

"Oh, she'll tell us." The man stepped closer to Grace, taking her arm and bringing it behind her. When she would have cried out, he jammed the barrel of a gun, hidden in his pocket, in her side. "Won't you, Grace?"

She gritted her teeth, willing her courage. Tossing back her head, she said, "I deal only with Kane."

"Kane's dead. Your mother's dead. It's just you and me, Grace."

A wave of blackness swept over Grace. The man grabbed one of her arms and Helen the other. They began to lead her out of the cenotaph.

Dead, Grace thought numbly. Her mother couldn't be dead. He was lying to her.

But as she glanced up at the man's cruel profile, she knew that he was not.

"Where are we going?" she asked weakly.

"You're going to take us to that tape. And if you decide to scream or make a scene, I'll shoot you dead where you stand."

"You're going to kill me anyway," Grace said breathlessly. "Why should I make it easier for you?"

"Because I can make it easy for you, or I can make it…fun. It's your choice."

She shuddered, envisioning the methods of torture

he would employ. "How can you do this?" she implored Helen desperately. "This man is a killer. He destroys lives. Why are you helping him?"

"You shouldn't have to ask me that question," Helen said coldly. "You know all about ambition, Grace. What a person will do to get what she wants. You're not so innocent."

Maybe Helen was right, Grace thought in despair. Maybe she was getting exactly what she deserved.

Outside, the cold air helped clear her senses. Grace glanced around, wondering what to do. They were going to kill her. She had no doubt about that. But if she screamed, drew a crowd, innocent bystanders could be hurt. If she didn't—

Several feet away, another group of sightseers had gathered around one of the granite markers set in the sidewalk, about fifty feet from the memorial. A man stood at the back of the group, towering over the others. Grace's heart began to race. Brady!

"Which way?" the man demanded.

Grace nodded down the street, to the pay telephone under which she'd fastened a blank tape. "That way."

He was still on one side of her, Helen on the other. Grace had to resist the urge to glance over her shoulder and see if Brady was following them.

At the pay phone, Grace said, "Here. It's taped underneath."

"Don't tell me—you were going to call Kane once you and your mother were safely away and tell him where the tape was. Kane would never have let you walk away.''

He gave her a little push toward the phone, and Grace knelt, unfastening the tape. She glanced down the street. She couldn't see Brady, but she knew he was there, waiting for an opportunity, a clean shot.

She held the tape out in her hand, and as Helen moved to take it, Grace grabbed her and lunged. They tumbled to the ground as the man fired. Helen had been struggling with Grace, but she suddenly went limp, a deadweight on top of Grace.

The man lifted his gun again, but before he could fire, Brady shouted, ''Kruger!''

Kruger, not Rialto—

He spun to fire, but Brady was quicker. He shot twice, and the man fell to the ground beside Grace.

She struggled to free herself from Helen's inert form. Brady helped her as pandemonium erupted on the street.

Grace was shaking all over. She looked down at her bloodstained clothes, then back up at Brady. ''My mother's dead,'' she whispered. ''She's dead.''

Brady took hold of her arms. ''No, Grace. She's alive. She's back at the hotel. She's going to be fine…Grace, did you hear what I said?''

Sobbing, Grace collapsed into Brady's arms.

THEY WERE MOVED to a secure suite with armed guards outside the door. A doctor was brought in to treat Angeline and to make sure Grace hadn't sustained any serious injuries. Everything had happened so quickly once the police arrived, Grace and Brady had become separated. He'd had someone take her back to the hotel while he talked to the police. She suspected he was also calling Mitchell Forbes.

Angeline was still sleeping, but the doctor had assured Grace there would be no lasting effects from the drug she'd been given. A nurse was with her round-the-clock, and after sitting by her mother's bedside for almost an hour, Grace finally tore herself away to shower and change clothes.

Physically exhausted and emotionally drained, she crawled into bed and had just drifted off when she heard her bedroom door open and close softly. A shadow moved stealthily across the room toward her.

"It's me," Brady whispered.

"I was hoping you'd come."

He sat down on the bed and leaned back against the headboard. Drawing her to him, he wrapped his arm around her and Grace closed her eyes, relishing the feel of him, the warmth of him.

"The man I shot was John Kruger," he said after a moment. "He was a DPS agent assigned to a drug task force in Houston. We don't know how long he's been working for Kane and Rialto, but we think he ultimately answers to Tomaso Calderone."

"And Helen?" Her friend's betrayal was still a deep ache inside Grace's heart.

"She and Kruger were lovers, the best we've been able to piece together. You must have gotten a little too close with some of your research, so Kruger became acquainted with Helen in order to keep tabs on you. After a while, she was willing to turn on you. I'm sorry, Grace.''

"I guess in some ways it serves me right," she said sadly. "Payback is hell, as they say."

He tightened his arm around her. "You didn't deserve what happened to you. None of it."

She sighed deeply. "Did you find Kane?"

"Yeah. He's...dead." He didn't elaborate, leaving Grace to imagine the condition in which the body had been found. John Kruger had been systematic. Other than Grace and the two bodyguards, who were now dead, Kane was the only one who could have placed the DPS agent in the warehouse that night.

She shuddered. "So what happens now?"

"Kane and Kruger are both dead, but that doesn't mean the danger is over for you. You've destroyed the alliance between Rialto and Kane. You've hurt Rialto's business. He's not likely to forget that."

Grace sat up in bed, staring at Brady. "You're saying my mother and I still have to disappear. We have to assume new identities, give up everything."

Brady's gaze seemed deep and unfathomable as he gazed back at her. "It's already being taken care of."

Grace got up from the bed and walked to the window to stare out. What were her choices here? She and her mother could leave the country and disappear, or they could enter the Witness Protection Program. Either way, she would never see Brady again.

He got up and came to stand behind her, placing his hands on her shoulders. "Your file will be classified at the highest level, but if security is ever breached, it'll show that Sara Granger and her mother, Eileen, are living in Portland Oregon."

"Portland," Grace whispered. So far away.

"And I'll go back to the ranch. Back to Texas Confidential, which is where I belong. Only, this time, I'll be going back with my wife."

Grace whirled, stunned. "Your wife?"

He smiled down at her, and her heart began to hammer almost painfully. "Your wife, Brady?"

"My wife, Catherine, and her mother." He lifted his hand to rub his knuckles down her face, and Grace caught his hand, holding it to her cheek.

"Tell me this isn't some cruel joke."

"You know me better than that." He drew her into his arms, holding her tight. "Although maybe I'm being a little too confident. Maybe I should ask first." He paused, his gaze enigmatic in the light from the street. "Will you marry me, Grace?"

She closed her eyes, reeling with emotion. "Oh, God, Brady, I never thought…I never dreamed…" She trailed off and gazed up at him solemnly. "Does this mean you forgive me?"

"Nothing to forgive. I told you once what's done is done. The slate is wiped clean. We have a chance to start all over again. And I do love you, Grace. You have to know that.''

"You don't know how long I've wanted to hear you say that."

"I think I have some idea. We belong together. Nothing is ever going to tear us apart again. I promise you that, Grace."

"Don't you mean Catherine?'' she teased.

"Might take awhile to get used to that," he said, pulling her toward the bed. They lay down side by side, still folded in each other's arms. "Cat. Cathy. Caty. Or just plain Catherine. What'll it be?"

"I don't care." Grace sighed happily. "At the moment, the only name I'm interested in is Mrs. Brady Morgan."

"I like the sound of that," he agreed.

And then for a long time, they didn't say anything at all.

*   *   *   *   *

We hope you enjoyed
THE BODYGUARD'S ASSIGNMENT
by Amanda Stevens.

Turn the page for a
sneak peek at the exciting
second book of Texas Confidential,

THE AGENT'S SECRET CHILD

by B.J. Daniels,
coming next month
from Harlequin Intrigue...

Chapter One

She smelled smoke. Just moments before, she'd been helping her daughter Elena look for her lost doll. Now, she stopped, alarmed. Her hand went to the small scars at her temple, memory of the fire and the pain sending panic racing through her. Why would Julio build a fire on such a hot spring day in Mexico?

Then she heard the raised voices below her in the kitchen and the heavy unfamiliar tread on the stairs.

The feeling came in a rush. Strong, sure, knowing, like only one she'd ever felt before. And yet she trusted this one. Whoever was coming up the stairs intended to harm her and her five-year-old daughter.

Fear paralyzed her as she realized she and Elena were trapped on the second floor. The only way out was the stairs the man now climbed. Her husband had barred the windows and he had the only key. She'd often wondered: What if there was another house fire and Julio wasn't home?

But Julio always left someone to watch over them when he was gone.

The lumbering footsteps reached the second floor landing. She shot her daughter a silent warning as she scooped the child into her arms and hurried to the attic stairs at the back of the house.

Her heart lunged in her chest as she moved through the hot, cluttered attic frantically searching for a place to hide. She found the only space large enough for the two of them in a dark corner behind an old bureau where the roof pitched out over the eave and a pile of old lumber formed a small partition.

She could hear the men ransacking the house, their voices raised in angry Spanish she couldn't make out.

When she heard the plodding tread on the attic stairs, she'd motioned to Elena to keep silent but the child's wide-eyed look told her that she understood their danger, just as she always had.

The man was in the attic now, moving slowly, carefully. The other men called to him, their feet thumping on the steps as they hurried up to him.

"Where is Isabella and the child?" one of the men demanded in Spanish. He had a quick, nervous voice like the bright-colored hummingbirds flickering in the Bougainvillea outside the window.

"I don't know," a deeper voice answered. "Montenegro must have gotten them out before we arrived."

"Damn Julio. Find the money. Tear the place apart but find the money."

"What if he gave it to her?" one of them asked, only to be answered with a curse.

As the men searched the house, she hugged her daughter tightly, determined to protect her child as she had since Elena's birth, feeling as defenseless and trapped as she always had.

The men eventually searched the attic, including the bureau drawers while she'd held her breath and prayed they wouldn't find her and Elena crouched in the darkness and dust.

She took hope when she sensed the men losing momentum, their movements less frantic but no less angry and frustrated.

"He wouldn't hide it in the house," one of the men snapped in Spanish. "He was too smart for that. So why are we wasting our time? He gave it to the woman and kid to hide somewhere for him."

"Shut up!" the nervous one growled. "Keep searching." But he said it as he tromped back down the stairs and soon the others followed.

She waited until she thought they'd left before she crept from the hiding place and stole with her daughter down a floor to her bedroom. With a chilling calm that frightened her more than the men had, she packed a bag with a few belongings.

She jumped at a noise behind her. Click, click, click. Someone was still downstairs, she thought, glancing at the phone beside her bed. It was making that faint clicking sound as the extension downstairs was being dialed.

With that same cold calm, she carefully picked up the extension. Two voices. One coarse as sand. The other nervous and quick and now familiar.

"I want my money, Ramon," the coarse one snarled.

"The woman must have taken it and the child with her."

"Find them. Make them tell you where Julio hid the money he stole from me. Then bring them and the money to me. *Comprendé?*"

"*Si*, Señor Calderone, I understand." The man named Ramon promised on his dead mother's grave.

She hung up the phone and finished packing. Since the day she'd awakened in the hospital after the house fire to find Julio beside her bed, she'd suspected her husband was involved with drug lord Tomaso Calderone.

She'd awakened in pain. From her injuries and the surgeries. From the confusion in her mind.

But it was awakening to find herself pregnant that made her close her eyes and ears to Julio's dealings, thinking only of her baby, her sweet precious daughter. Julio had never shown any interest in either of them, leaving her alone to cook and clean and raise the child he wanted nothing to do with.

Once she got some of her strength back physically and Elena was old enough to travel, she'd tried to leave her marriage. But Julio had caught her and brought her back, warning her that she and Elena could never leave. They were his and he would rather see them both dead than ever let them go.

She had looked into Julio Montenegro's eyes and known then that he felt nothing for her or Elena, something she had long suspected. She and Elena were his prisoners for reasons she could not understand. But for Elena's sake, she'd never tried to escape again.

Instead, without realizing it, she'd been biding her time, waiting. She hadn't known what she'd been waiting for. Until today.

With the bag in one hand and Elena's small hand in the other, she crept down the stairs as soon as the lower floor grew silent again.

Julio lay sprawled on the white kitchen tile in a pool of blood, his eyes blank, his body lifeless.

Shielding Elena from the sight, Isabella moved to him, her gaze not on his face, but the knife sticking out of his chest.

With a cold calculating detachment she hadn't known she possessed, she grasped the knife handle in both hands, and pulled it from her husband's chest. Then she calmly wiped the knife clean on his shirt and slipped the slim blade into her bag.

She looked down at his face for a moment, wishing she felt something. Then, like a sleepwalker, she knelt and searched his pockets, lifting him enough to remove the small wad of pesos his business associates had obviously passed up as too trivial to bother with in his hip pocket.

It wasn't much money. Not near enough to get

her and Elena out of Mexico, let alone to someplace safe in the States. But was there anyplace safe from Calderone and his men?

She started to rise, then noticed that when she'd lifted Julio, she'd also lifted the edge of the rug under him. The corner of a manila envelope was now visible beneath the rug.

With that same chilling calm, she raised Julio enough to free the parcel from beneath him and the rug. She stared at the large manila envelope, then the fire he'd built in the stove. Had he been planning to burn the envelope? Why else would he have built a fire in a room already unbearably hot?

She looked again at the envelope. She knew it didn't contain the missing money. It was too light-weight, too thin, to hold the amount of money she feared Julio had stolen. But maybe it had information about where he'd hidden the drug money. Why else would he try to burn it just before he'd been killed if not to protect his ill-gotten gains?

She grasped onto the hope. If she had the location of the stolen money, then maybe she could buy her freedom and her daughter's from Calderone.

As she lifted the parcel to look inside, something fell out and tinkled to the tiles. The tiny object rolled to a stop and as she stooped to pick it up, she saw that it was a silver heart-shaped locket. It had no chain and the silver was tarnished and scratched, making it hard at first to read the name engraved on it.

Abby.

She stared at the locket. Should that name mean something to her? Was it one of her husband's mistresses? One of her lost relatives?

She pried the two halves open and stared down at a man's photo inside, her fingers trembling. Not Julio. Not any man she'd ever seen before. She felt Elena beside her and tried to shield her from the body on the floor, but saw that her daughter was more interested in the locket—and the photo inside.

"Papacito," Elena whispered, eyes wide as she stared down at the photo of the stranger.

"No, my little bright angel," she said softly, sick inside. For the first time, she let herself hate Julio. She'd never wanted him as a husband, but he could have been a father to Elena, who desperately needed a father's love.

Instead their daughter preferred to believe a total stranger in a small black and white photograph was her father rather than Julio Montenegro, the unfeeling father who'd given her life.

A car backfired outside, making her jump. Hurriedly, she shoved the locket into the envelope with the official looking papers. Like the weapon she'd taken from Julio's chest, she put the parcel into her bag. As she turned to leave, she saw her daughter's lost rag doll and, wondering absently how it had gotten there, she scooped it up from the floor, took her daughter's small hand, and ran.

JAKE CANTRELL stood back, sipping his beer, watching the wedding reception as if through binoculars.

The Smoking Barrel Ranch had taken on a sound and feel and level of gaiety that seemed surreal as if it had an alternate personality—one he didn't recognize.

He hadn't been brought here for this and right now, he just wanted it to be over. Not that he wasn't happy for Brady and Grace…now Catherine. He was. He just didn't believe in happily ever after anymore. Mostly, he told himself, he was just anxious to get back to work.

But that was a lie. All day he'd felt an uneasiness he couldn't shake. Like when he felt someone following him or waiting for him in a dark alley. The feeling hummed like a low-pitched vibration inside him, making him anxious and irritable and wary.

Mitchell had called a meeting later tonight. Jake wanted a new assignment, something that would take him away from the ranch for a while. Away from everything. Work kept him sane—relatively sane. It was also the only thing that kept him from dwelling on the past.

He felt eyes on him. Not just watching him. But staring at him. He shifted his gaze and saw Penny Archer across the room standing with her back to the library door she'd just closed behind her. Earlier he'd noticed when she'd gotten a beep on the priority line. Noting was something he was good at. That and finding people who didn't want to be found.

It had to have been a business call, the only kind that would make the administrative assistant leave the wedding reception and the boisterous crowd, and disappear into the library and the hidden elevator that would take her to the basement and the secret office of Texas Confidential. The true heart of the ranch. Its aberrant split personality.

Now he met Penny's intent gaze and felt a jolt. She was as tough as they came. It took a lot to upset her. And right now, she was visibly upset.

He made his way across the room, knowing it had been the priority call that had upset her. Just as he knew the call had to do with him.

"What?" he asked, never one to mince words.

She motioned for him to follow and led him away from the crowd and the noise of the party, outside to a corner of the porch. In the distance, mesquite stood dark-limbed against the horizon, shadows piled cool and deep beneath them. The land beyond as vast and open as the night sky.

"I just got the strangest call," she said the moment they were alone and out of earshot. Her gaze came up to his. "It was from a little girl. A child. No more than three or four. She spoke Spanish and—" Penny's voice broke. "She was crying. She sounded really scared, Jake."

"What did she want?" he asked, wondering what this could possibly have to do with him.

"She said her mommy was in trouble and needed help. She asked for her daddy." Penny seemed to hesitate. "Her daddy Jake."

He felt a chill even as a warm Texas wind whispered through the May night. He shook his head. A mistake. A wrong number. An odd coincidence.

"Jake, she called through your old FBI contact number."

He stared, his heart now a sledgehammer. Only three people in the world had ever known that number and two of them were dead. "What did she say? Exactly." Not that he had to add that. Penny could remember conversations verbatim. That was part of her charm—and the reason the thirty-four-year-old was Mitchell Forbes right-hand woman.

She repeated the Spanish words. "Then I heard a woman's voice in the background. The woman cried, 'No, *chica suena.*' Then the line went dead. Of course, I put a trace on the call immediately. It came from a small motel on the other side of the Mexican border."

Chica suena. The light in the trees seemed to shift. Lighter to darker. The porch under him no longer solid. A swampland of deadly potholes. His world, the fragile one he'd made for himself here, spun on the edge of out of control. Just as it had six years ago. Before Mitchell had saved him.

From far off, he heard Penny ask, "Jake, are you all right? Jake?"

Chica suena. He hadn't heard the unusual Spanish endearment in years. Six long years. Nor was it one he'd ever heard before he'd met Abby Diaz. It was something her grandmother had called her. It meant *my little dream girl.* And it suited Abby.

Abby Diaz had been everything to him. The

woman he was to marry. His FBI partner. His most trusted friend.

His *chica suena*.

He bounded off the porch, his long legs carrying him away from the party and the faint sound of music and laughter. Away from the pain and anger and memory of the death of his dreams of love ever after. Away. But he knew gut-deep that running wouldn't help. It never had.

Someone had found out about him and Abby. Had found out their most intimate secret. Daddy Jake. *Chica suena.* Someone wanted him running scared again. And they'd succeeded.

THE SECRET IS OUT!

HARLEQUIN®

INTRIGUE®

presents

**By day these agents are cowboys;
by night they are specialized
government operatives.
Men bound by love, loyalty and the law—
they've vowed to keep their missions
and identities confidential....**

Harlequin Intrigue

Harlequin American Romance
(a special tie-in story)

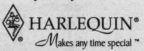

HARLEQUIN®
Makes any time special ™

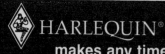

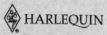

HARLEQUIN

INTRIGUE®

COMING NEXT MONTH

#585 THE AGENT'S SECRET CHILD by BJ Daniels
Texas Confidential

FBI agent Jake Cantrell thought his partner and lover Abby Diaz died in an explosion following a failed mission. But when he got a call from a little girl claiming to be his daughter *and* was assigned to find a beautiful and all-too-familiar stranger, he wasn't so sure. Can he unlock the secrets of the mystery woman's past, along with her heart, before it's too late?

#586 CRADLE WILL ROCK by Susan Kearney
The Sutton Babies

After Laura Embry was framed for murder, she fled Colorado never knowing she carried Chase Sutton's baby. But Chase wasn't the kind of man to let her go without a fight. And when he learned he had a child to protect as well as the woman he loved…there wasn't anything he wouldn't do to clear Laura's name.

#587 HER MYSTERIOUS STRANGER by Debbi Rawlins
Secret Identity

When bounty hunter and missing persons expert Taryn Scott teamed up with handsome, illusive lawyer Nick Travis, she uncovered more than she bargained for and fell headlong into danger. Trouble was, she couldn't figure out what was more threatening—the secrets she uncovered or her feelings for Nick!

#588 ONE GOOD MAN by Julie Miller

Traumatized after a vicious attack, Casey Maynard withdrew from society and vowed she'd trust no one. Not even her bodyguard, Mitch Taylor. Now her stalker had escaped and was on the loose! Mitch swore he'd stop at nothing to protect Casey, but who would protect his heart?

Visit us at www.eHarlequin.com

CNM0900